DEFINING CHANCES

A CANDLEWOOD FALLS NOVEL

STACEY WILK

TITLE

Copyright © 2022 by Stacey Wilk

Cover design copyright © 2025 by Jen Talty

ISBN: (ebook edition) **978-1-7364714-6-3**

ISBN: (paperback edition) **978-1-7364714-7-0**

Printed in the USA

For Loren
My true blue

PRAISE FOR STACEY WILK'S BOOKS

Through the Darkness "Wilk pens a heart gripping story that will leave you breathless." *Jen Talty, USA Today Bestselling Author*

The Essence of Whiskey and Tea: "If you enjoy a good series about family and love, then this novel is sure to soothe your soul." *Booktrib*

Time Won't Erase: "The power of redemption shines in this emotional story about second chances." *Caridad Pineiro, New York Times and USA Today Bestselling Author*

Taking Root: "...multiple layers of entertainment." *InD'Tale Magazine*

Whispering Christmas: "She makes you feel deeply for each character as if you a part of the Candlewood Falls family." *Mint Copy Services*

Defining Chances: The author masterfully weaves together real-life situations, creating a narrative that's both thought-provoking and emotionally resonant. You'll find yourself rooting for Ember and Raf as they navigate their troubled pasts and learn to let go of guilt and anger.
Hidden Gems Reviews

HAVE WE GOT A STORY FOR YOU!

Dear Readers:

Welcome to Candlewood Falls!

Each Candlewood Falls book stands alone. However, the end of one story doesn't mean the end of your favorite characters. They can show up in any Candlewood Falls book at any time!

Candlewood Falls is a unique world of connected stories by different authors whose characters, businesses, and events appear in each others' novels.

Think of Candlewood Falls as a literary soap opera!

Be sure to check out the Ready For Another Trip to Candlewood Falls page at the end to discover which other books include your favorite characters.

Happy reading!

Stacey Wilk, K.M Fawcett, & Jen Talty

CHAPTER ONE

E mber Wilde sat on the floor of the New York City apartment she couldn't afford, holding her phone and shaking. She had to go home. Right now. In fact, she should have left sooner. Throwing some things into an overnight bag, she locked up the apartment and shot off an email to her boss. She wouldn't be back. Ever. She hated that job anyway.

Out on the concrete, the traffic noise bumped into her like an oversized marching band of car horns, ambulance sirens, and squealing brakes. She was tired of the dirt and crowds of the city, anyway. Keith could keep the apartment. She sent him a text as she caught the C train to midtown.

You can move back in. Moving out. I'll come back for my stuff.

What? her ex sent in return.

I'm going home. Her mother needed her.

Another rash decision. Keith's words almost vibrated off

the screen. He had always accused her of acting first and thinking second—of running away.

Not rash. Important. More important than he knew because family never mattered to him.

I don't want to move back in so you can change your mind again. Keith would never forgive her for breaking them up twice, but the first time she had been scared of the idea of making it on her own. She had only taken him back after he begged.

I won't. She couldn't stay married to a man like her father, so the divorce had been finalized.

How long will you be gone?

For good. She shoved her phone into her purse. She didn't want to read anything more from him or have to explain that her mother was doing worse, or that her father wasn't taking care of her properly. At least that's what her older sister Petra had said on the phone.

The subway pulled into Penn Station. Ember jumped onto a train headed for Candlewood Falls. Her father would be displeased with her arrival. Not that she cared. She had been a source of displeasure for her father since the second the doctor announced she was a girl. Huck Wilde had wanted boys and fathered three girls instead. Poetic justice in her book.

As much as she and Huck didn't get along, she loved her mother. Ruby was a vibrant woman—before her illness—who enjoyed laughing and baking. She was quickly becoming less than herself now, forgetting her keys or how to get back home from the grocery store. Sometimes she stumbled over her words, like yesterday in the check-out line, according to Petra.

Her father was failing her mother, and that wasn't

okay. Ember would find a way to fix things, although her father would fight her at each and every step. He liked things his way. Ember would take care of her mother. Her father could learn to deal with it.

The train approached the Candlewood Falls stop. She and her sisters had scattered from the small town set in the rolling hills of New Jersey because there wasn't anything here for a young person who wanted a big career. Working at the family business had never been her dream, not that she was living her dream as a computer programmer either. She also left because residing near her father would have driven her mad.

She grabbed her bag and descended to the platform, which wasn't much more than a sidewalk. Some other people left the train with her, hurrying to their next destination or accepting hugs from someone waiting. People milled around the station made of stone with their faces planted in their phones. A few cars dotted the parking lot. She hadn't expected so much activity at the little train station.

The afternoon sun sat high in the sky like a yellow ball in mid-bounce, though the clouds rolling in from the west threatened to interfere with its fun. For all her determination to stay away—which she had for many years—today she had effectively rendered herself homeless, jobless, and back to the place it all started.

The ride request app stated a driver was more than thirty minutes away. No surprise there. Everything in Hunterdon County was at least that far away from the next location unless someone wanted a horse farm or an orchard. Those were on every corner. She could walk, but that might take an hour or more. She was not about to notify her father she was in town until she arrived at the house. She needed surprise on her side. Besides, he'd just drive her right back to the city once he had her in his truck.

She could call her cousins Brad or Brooklyn, but they hadn't spoken in ages. She couldn't exactly ask for a last-minute favor. She hadn't spoken to her other cousins, Lacey and Sam, in even longer. That left her Uncle Silas, but she wasn't sure if the man who lived up the mountain without indoor plumbing even had a phone.

"Looks like you're walking," she said under her breath and shoved her phone in her purse.

"Excuse me?" The male voice next to her made her jump.

"What did you say?" She hadn't realized anyone was standing so close. She might have liked being more prepared for the smoldering gaze from close-set eyes that met hers. This tall man with jet-black hair and a strong jaw set her off-balance.

"You said something, no?" The navy-blue polo shirt stretched its satiny fabric over his muscles. He had a surfer's body, sculpted and lean.

"No. I mean, I did, but I wasn't speaking with you. I was talking to myself." But too loudly, if the stranger five feet away could hear her. She'd have to mumble better next time.

"Have we met?" He narrowed his eyes.

Just what she needed, some guy to hit on her now. "I don't believe so. Excuse me." She stepped around him, dragging her bag behind her. She'd walk for a while. Then she'd break down and call Brooklyn. Hopefully, her cousin would take pity on her and give her a ride.

Most of the family felt sorry for her and her sisters because of all the Wilde brothers that owned the orchard, she, Petra, and Nyx were stuck with Huck. She'd have to capitalize on a little of that pity in the form of a ride.

"Ember, right? You're Ember Wilde." The dark and handsome man, who reminded her of a younger Andy Garcia, called after her. His lips curled up and revealed a bright, confident smile.

"Who told you that?" In Candlewood Falls, the sleepy small town where everyone knew everyone else, there was no point in denying her identity, though she didn't know his. If she were in the city, she would be reaching for the key chain where she kept her Mace or at the very least her phone, and she would not admit to being anyone. But his relaxed stance and easy demeaner said he wasn't a threat.

"It's Rafael Alvarez." The expression on his face suggested she should know that.

But the man in front of her did not match the image planted in her memory of the boy she had went to high school with. They had not been friends back then, but in Candlewood Falls it would be hard not to be familiar with one another.

"Right. Of course. You still work at Wilde Orchards." Every once in a while her mother would share some stories about the orchard. Rafael's name would pop up. She still couldn't get over how he had filled out, nicely she might add, the bones in his face more pronounced. If memory served, in school he was rail thin as if he hardly ate. Now, he appeared strong and fit.

"I do. I'm sure you hear this all the time, but wow, you look just like Huck."

"Thanks, I think." Heat fanned her cheeks. Her father was a handsome man, but what was on the inside counted. Most people tolerated Huck. That couldn't make his outward appearance enjoyable.

"It was a compliment. I recognized you because he showed me a picture. You have those Wilde blue eyes everyone in the family has." He held out a hand. His smile was disarming.

She didn't even know her father had a picture of her, never mind one that he showcased. She hesitated for a second. Rafael noticed her eyes. Observant for an almost stranger.

His outstretched hand waited, leaving her little choice except to slide hers inside his large calloused grip. His skin was warm and for the first time since her call with Petra, some of the chill left her bones.

"It was nice to see you again, but I have to go. I have a long walk if I'm going to get to my parents' house sometime today." She pulled her hand away because if she held on any longer, she might not let go until her whole body had stopped shivering.

"You can't walk to Huck's from here. Let me give you a ride. My truck is right over there." He hitched a thumb over his shoulder.

"No, thank you." She turned to go.

"Stubborn like him too." Raf slid into step beside her.

"What are you doing?" She stumbled, but yanked her bag whose wheels wouldn't cooperate and kept going.

This man had another thing coming if he thought he would walk with her.

"Going for a walk." He ignited that smile. His teeth were small and perfect.

Did the orchard always employ such handsome men? Of course, she had no idea. She hadn't been to the orchard in years.

She had left for college and never came back. There had been nothing here for her. Her mother had always come into the city to visit, leaving her father behind who always complained work needed his attention. *Those apples don't grow themselves*, he had said. As if there wasn't plenty of help to grow a stupid apple or two.

"You're not walking with me." She forced the bubble of laughter down. She didn't want to encourage him and picked up her speed. She might have to run if those clouds continued to move in. Even the breeze had picked up, blowing her hair away from her face.

"There's no law that says I can't go for a stroll." His long legs matched hers with ease. He shoved his hands in his pockets and whistled a tune.

"I don't want you to walk with me." But she did like the whistling.

"It's far, and there aren't any sidewalks. The sun will set soon. You could end up in a ditch."

She stopped. "You don't owe me any favors just because you work with my father. I'm a grown-up. I can manage the very dangerous streets of Candlewood Falls." She didn't need some man thinking she needed saving. And definitely not a man who worked at the orchard.

"Suit yourself." He shrugged and turned around.

"Enjoy your walk. It's about seven miles," he said over his shoulder.

"Thanks. I will." The first fat raindrop plopped on her head. She turned. "Hey, Rafael, I do need to ask you something."

His smile took a slow amble across his face. "You want the ride."

"No, it's not that. Would you mind not mentioning to anyone at the orchard that you saw me until I speak to my parents?" For all she knew he would be on the phone to her father giving away her advantage. She wished she had arranged for a car. The next raindrop landed on her nose.

"You don't have to worry about that. Huck and I only speak when necessary. You better get moving. The rain is coming." He jogged off to the parking lot, leaving her on the side of the road underneath the raindrops.

Well, she had asked him to leave her alone. If she had wanted the ride, she should have said so. But she hadn't wanted to seem needy, and though her instincts said he was safe, she didn't think it was a good idea to get in a car with a strange man—albeit not completely unknown.

He pulled out of the parking lot and passed her with a wave. She offered a half-hearted wave back, regretting her decision to walk, and gripped the bag's handle to resume her poorly executed quest. But the clouds had the final laugh and poured their contents on her head.

CHAPTER TWO

Raf kicked himself for leaving Ember Wilde on the side of the road in the pouring rain, but she had insisted she didn't need his help. Another independent woman determined to prove it at all costs. Including getting soaked and probably freezing. That tan sweater and denim jacket she wore well weren't exactly waterproof.

But he had learned his lesson with women. Stay away. That was easier than getting slapped for holding open a door. If his Spanish grandmother were still alive, he'd have to break her heart and tell her all that advice about standing when a woman entered the room or bringing her flowers didn't work. He didn't understand why women believed because he was trying to show them respect he was also insulting their independence. Nothing was sexier than a woman who knew what she wanted and went after it by herself.

He pulled into Wilde Orchards and parked in the back. He had been working at this orchard since he was a scrawny kid in desperate need of caring for his younger brothers. And every time he set foot on the property, his lungs filled with good air. He had helped build this place, and all the thriving apple trees were a testament to that.

He gave a wave to the employees behind the register as he walked through the store where they sold apples and baked goods, along with some Wilde Orchards clothing, and to the employee area where the offices were situated.

Brad, his boss and best friend, had sent a text a half hour ago saying he needed to talk. Because Brad was the vice president of operations and the grandson of the president, nothing went on at the orchard that Brad didn't know about. Raf suspected Brad wanted to talk about the new pesticides for the apple trees. The organic ones cost more, but they were worth it.

He knocked but didn't wait to enter. "What's going on?"

He stopped dead in his tracks. Brad sat at his desk, which took up most of the space in the office, with a snarl painted across his face. Brad was a big guy and usually with only a look he could wither the toughest of men. But it wasn't the snarl that worried him. It was the reason why.

Raf's brother Tino sat on the other side of the desk, staring at his hands in his lap.

"What did you do now?" He shoved Tino's shoulder. Tino was the youngest of the four brothers and the one always in trouble. Raf had spent most of Tino's life getting him out of said trouble. At twenty-six, Tino still behaved like an angry teenager, and Raf was sick of it.

Tino shrugged.

"What did he do?" He turned to Brad. He would beat the living daylights out of his brother for this one. He had sworn to Brad right before Christmas that Tino wouldn't be a problem. Now, Tino had made him a liar. All he had wanted was for his brother to finally get his life in order, but he was always screwing up.

"He stole." Brad glared at Tino.

"What?" The wind went out of him. He leaned against the wall to catch his breath and keep from toppling over. Instead, he bumped into a picture of Brad and him on a hunting trip some years back.

"Do you want to tell him or are you going to make me do it?" Brad pushed out of the chair and stood his full height.

If he had been Tino, he would have been shaking in his boots. Tino only shrugged again.

"Fine. Take the coward's way out." Brad turned to him. "I'm sorry, man. He got caught skimming money from the applesauce deliveries."

He lunged across the room and pulled Tino out of the chair, shaking him. Tino's eyes rolled into the back of his head. "You took money from the people who feed you? You stole from my family? What the hell is the matter with you?"

Brad gripped him by the shoulders and pushed him away from Tino. "Knock it off. You"—he turned to Tino—"sit. Raf, you okay?" Brad stepped back, taking a deep breath.

"I'm going to kill you." He ducked around Brad to get to Tino, but Brad shoved him hard, bouncing him off the wall. The picture clattered to the ground.

"Enough. If beating the shit out of him would help, I

would have done it already. I called you to come in because I wanted you to find out here with me in the room before I call the police. Otherwise, he'd already be at the station." Brad retrieved the photo and tossed it on the desk.

"You're going to have him arrested?" He might want to put a big hurt on his kid brother, but Tino couldn't go back to jail. That would kill him for sure.

"I don't have a choice. Huck caught him. If it had been my dad or my grandfather, or even Sam, I could have stopped it. But Huck's waiting at home for me to call him and tell him it's done or he's going to do it himself. I can't let Huck turn him in. Huck has too much influence with the police force. What you would do to Tino would be nothing."

"I'm sitting right here. Don't talk about me like I'm not." Tino shifted in his seat.

"Shut up." Raf pointed a finger at Tino, then turned to Brad. "You can't report him. He's violated his parole. He'll be in jail for good. And even if you turn him in yourself, all Huck has to do is make a call. He'll be at Rahway in hours. Please, Brad, let me deal with him."

Brad pulled him out into the hallway and shut the door. "Raf, man, you promised me he wouldn't cause any trouble."

"I know. I'm sorry. I thought he had changed. I'll pay back whatever he took. I'll work around the clock to make it right. You can dock my pay, whatever you want. Just please, let me deal with him myself. I can't let him go to jail. He's my kid brother."

"You can't keep fixing things for him." Brad leaned against the wall and pushed the hair out of his face.

"Just this last time. I'll get him into therapy. I'll figure something out." He had no idea how to make Tino straighten up. He had tried to beg him, help him, beat him up, nothing worked. Tino was still angry because their mother had died when he was just a toddler. Raf, Matias, and Axel had been teens. Without their mother, not that she was any prize, they were left with his useless father until the day he walked out and disappeared.

"Raf, man, I can't have anyone else who works here thinking they should try it too."

"Fire me."

"Excuse me?" Brad's eyebrows climbed to his hairline.

"Fire me. I'll walk away from the orchard with Tino. You don't send him to jail, and the guys don't lose respect for you. I can't let that happen either." The solution wasn't perfect, but it was the best he could come up with on short notice. He didn't want to let Brad down, but he had to save Tino somehow.

"You've lost your mind. I'm not going to fire you for something your brother did. I do want to punch you for talking me into letting him come on board, but I can't fire you. You're my right-hand man, and we have plans for Friday night."

His brother Axel's unveiling. He almost forgot. He wouldn't miss it. He wouldn't let another brother down because somewhere along the way he had let Tino down. "I have to protect Tino from jail. I'll drag him into therapy. Please let me figure it out."

"I'm sorry, man, but your brother is a loser. Don't waste any more of your life on him. Let him pay for his mistakes."

"Hey, I'm all he's got. I can't leave him flapping in the wind. I won't let him end up dead which will happen if he goes to jail. Do you hear me? I can't let my little brother die in prison." He had lost his mother when he was fifteen. For years, he assumed his father was dead too, but he knew now that Johnny Alvarez walked the earth somewhere. He could not lose Tino. He wouldn't survive that.

Brad wiped a hand over his face. "Shit. Okay, for you because you're the brother I don't have. Get Tino as far from here as you can. Get him out of town. I'll deal with Huck. But for the record, Tino should go to jail."

He ignored Brad's last comment about Tino. "Thank you. I owe you big-time. I'll pay you back every penny he stole. You'll never have to deal with him again. I swear."

Brad grabbed him in a rough hug. "You're crazy."

"I have to help him." He had been taking care of all his brothers since their father left when he was eighteen. He had to get Tino on the right road somehow.

"I'm here if you need me." Brad shoved him away and opened the door. "Tino, get your shit and get out of here. You owe your brother. You better find a way to repay him."

"What did you do with the money?" Raf made a sharp turn into his driveway. The truck bucked over the asphalt. Tino hadn't said a word the whole way back. The rain pelted the windshield, making it difficult to see or his vision was blurred by fury. An errant thought popped into his head. He hoped Ember Wilde had found herself a ride and hadn't walked in the rain. When Huck found out Tino didn't go to prison for stealing, he would hate the Alvarezes more than he already did.

"It's gone." Tino stared out the window.

Of course it was. Tino probably spent it on booze. "How much?"

"I don't know."

"Well, figure it out. I'm going to pay the Wildes back and you are going to work off the debt somehow to pay me back. And you're going into therapy tomorrow."

"Yeah, right. Therapy doesn't work."

"Tell me why, Santino. Tell me why you would steal from the Wildes of all people." They had been the reason Raf could keep his brothers out of foster care. They had been the people who had believed in him when no one else did. The pain of embarrassment squeezing his chest made him grip the wheel harder. He would have to call Brad's dad, Silas, and apologize. Silas had been a second father to him when he needed one most.

"Because they have it all, and we have nothing. And you're so busy kissing all their asses like they're gods or something." Tino shoved out of the truck into the rain without a look back. He didn't seem to care the rain soaked through his shirt and plastered his hair to his head. Tino didn't care about a whole lot and that had always been the problem.

Tino went through the front door on the left side of the duplex that Raf owned. Tino lived on one side while Raf lived in the other. He had bought this house years ago because the bank trusted the Wildes. His whole life had been wrapped up in that family. They had taken him in, and he had made them his own. Other than his three brothers, he had no one. And now Tino may have damaged that relationship beyond repair.

Just once he wished they had a father he could count on. Just once he didn't want to have to take care of Tino alone.

CHAPTER THREE

E mber stamped her soaking wet feet on the porch of her parents' old farmhouse. She had walked the whole way from the train station in the rain. Cold raindrops had run down her neck and under her sweater. Puddles filled her shoes. She was pretty sure everything in her bag was soaked too. It was a little too late, but she wished she had taken that ride.

She paused with her fisted hand near the door. She had a key. This had been her home once, but it didn't feel like it anymore. She was a stranger here at this house and in Candlewood Falls. Nothing was the same. Not her, not this place, and certainly not her mother.

She knocked and held her breath. Lumbering footsteps echoed on the other side of the door with the glass top covered in a lacy cream curtain. Her mother loved delicate things. Her father was anything but.

The door opened on a creaky hinge. Her father stood before her. He was tall and thin, but his shoulders hunched some now and his hair was white and cut close to his head. The haircut hadn't changed. He didn't like any hair length on men and said as much whenever he could. Her cousin Brad had hair to his shoulders. Her dad must grunt and groan every time he saw him.

Dad's blue eyes, the eyes that Rafael had noticed, were hooded and red. The lines on his face and neck had deepened. For the first time, he appeared old to her, not the scary man who shouted loud enough to shake the roof when things didn't go his way.

"Well, I'll be. Ember Rose. What are you doing here?" Her father always liked to use her middle name even though she never did.

"Hi, Dad. Can I come in?" She didn't want to have the conversation she needed to have with him while she stood dripping wet on the porch. She'd love to make a hot cup of tea or cocoa, even though it was April and not the dead of winter, to chase the dampness out of her bones.

"Soaked like that? Why are you wet? And you brought a suitcase? What for? You planning on packing up those old dolls in the attic finally?" He didn't budge from his spot blocking the doorway.

"I got caught in the rain." As if that wasn't obvious. "I've come for a visit. If that's all right."

Her sister Petra had warned her that their father wasn't agreeable to any visits from his daughters. He didn't want anyone interfering with the care he was giving their mother, but Petra had said the house was a mess and Mom seemed worse than when she had come for Easter a few weeks ago.

Petra had wanted to stay, but her daughter needed to get back for school. Their sister Nyx was on tour with her band and couldn't get away. That left Ember. And when Petra had explained about Mom forgetting her words in the store, she had found herself shaking on the floor of her apartment wanting, no needing, to do something to help her mother. Sitting still was never her strong suit.

"After all this time, you just decided to stop by? What kind of a fool do you think I am? Your sister put you up to this. I knew Petra would be on the phone before she could pull out of the driveway. She's always meddling, that one. Well, you don't have to worry. Things are just fine here."

"Petra doesn't know I'm here." No one did except for Rafael. At least he had held up his promise not to give her father a heads-up about her arrival. Maybe that had been a bad idea. Maybe if her father had had a few minutes to digest her inevitable arrival, he would have had time to simmer down. And maybe, just maybe if she had shown up with Rafael, her father might have withheld some of his disapproval in front of a non-family member.

"Huck, who's at the door?" Her mother's familiar voice called out from the back of the house, except it didn't hold the usual vibrancy. The words shook like paper in the wind, and the projection was low and soft like a feather pillow.

"Stay back there, Ruby. I've got this."

"It's me, Mom." She stood on her toes and leaned around her father to make sure her voice carried down the long hall. She would not be bullied into leaving.

"Ember, sweetheart, you're home." Mom shuffled down the hall in her knit pants and oversized sweater.

She wore a scarf—her signature piece—in a fancy knot around her neck. Her hair was completely gray and cut short, but stylish. Her smile was wide and recognition brewed in her eyes.

Mom was having a good day. Ember pushed past her father and dripped on the floor as she folded her mom into a hug. Mom's familiar vanilla scent enveloped her. Tears pricked behind her eyes. She held on to her mom as if she might blow away. Mom held on as tightly.

"You're all wet." Mom pulled out of the embrace and gave her the once-over. "Did you miss the bus?"

"She's not in school, Ruby." Huck huffed and shook his head. "She's over forty now."

Mom stared at Dad with her mouth hanging open, but rearranged her face like a flash. "I know that, Huck. I can see she's not a child." Mom turned to her. "Let's get you changed. You must be freezing. Why were you out in the rain?"

Mom went down the hall and into the kitchen that sat at the back of the house. The kitchen was white and old with appliances that hadn't been replaced in thirty years. The wood floor planks were worn from the abuse of abrasive footsteps.

The heat blasted from of the old-style radiators, drying all the moisture out of the room and her throat. The farmhouse-style sink was filled with dirty dishes. The drying rack was stacked with clean plates and a couple of pots. Her father had never installed a dishwasher for her mother. The counter could use a few minutes with a sponge and the garbage needed taking out.

"I came to see how you're doing. I'm going to

change." She tossed her jacket on the washing machine in the laundry room off the kitchen, then slipped into the small half-bath. The toilet needed a good wipe and the dust was an inch thick on every flat surface, but it could be worse. She struggled with opening her suitcase in the small space.

Most of her clothes were just damp. She peeled off her jeans and dried her legs with the hand towel hanging by the sink. She pulled on a dry sweatshirt and a pair of leggings. At least she wasn't shivering as much. She could use a little of the heat that had rolled off Rafael in waves.

She chuckled to herself. Any kind of thoughts about an attractive and hot man were pointless at the moment. She wasn't in the market for another relationship. She was in town to see to it that her mother was taken care of while she figured out what she wanted to do with her life.

She gripped the sink and stared in the mirror. She had no job and no place to live. Her life was a mess and she had no idea how to fix it. Coming to Candlewood Falls wasn't going to do that for her. And after a few days of living with her parents, would she really be able to stay around? If her father was as impossible as Petra had said—and by the way he greeted her at the door, it sure appeared that way—he would fight her on every-thing she tried to do. Tears burned her eyes again. Coming here without a plan was a very bad idea. When would she learn to think first and act second?

A knock came at the door. "Ember, I made you some tea," Mom said. "Hurry up before it gets cold."

With a long heavy breath, she left the sanctuary of the tiny bathroom.

Her parents sat at the kitchen table. An extra cup was set for her. Her mother stared out the window. Her father glared at her.

"Warm yourself up. Get your clothes dried. Then I'll drive you back to the train," her father said.

"You're leaving already?" Mom looked between her and her father.

"No."

"Yes," her father said at the same time.

"I'd like to spend a few days here. You can put up with me that long, can't you, Dad?" She took the seat and gripped the mug, keeping her gaze directly on her father's. She couldn't back down now. He had thrown the challenge out. She had to hold her ground for once.

"Suit yourself. We already had dinner. If you were planning on eating, you'll have to make it or you can go into town." Her father pushed out of the chair and disappeared through the doorway. A door closed in the distance with a snap.

Her father had retired to his study. Not that he spent a lot of time reading or writing. The room was once a small parlor that faced the side of the house and now held nothing more than a scratched-up desk and worn-out leather chair. She knew of some of the things her father orchestrated behind that door. Nothing she approved of. He belonged to a local group of men who fancied themselves an organization that brought order to Candlewood Falls. Instead, they brought division and hatred.

She turned to her mother. "How are you feeling?"

"Fine. How are you feeling?" Mom stirred a spoon in her tea, clicking the metal against the porcelain.

"Better now." She was glad to see her mother having such a good day, but she had no idea what she was going to do with her when things went south. But whatever she decided, she couldn't do any worse than what her father had been doing. And from the looks of the kitchen, he wasn't even keeping house.

Mom gripped her hand. "Ember, sweetheart, I'm so glad you came home. But it might be better for everyone if you didn't stay long. I don't want your father upset. He's been through a lot lately."

"What about you? You've been through more." Her insides burned. Her mother constantly put her husband's needs above her own. She had to make her mother understand that in these next months, maybe years, her needs had to be a priority over her husband's.

"Don't worry about me. I'm tougher than I look. But your father, he can't handle the stress of what's been happening. Work is picking up at the orchard too. There was a bit of a problem there the other day. I think. He wouldn't say exactly, but... Oh, what's his name...?" Mom squeezed her eyes shut. "Bradford. Yes, Bradford. Silas's son. Bradford called about something and upset your father. He wouldn't say what it was except it had to do with work."

Her mother had struggled to regain her nephew's name. Her heart ached. "He's a grown man. He can put up with a few inconveniences, including me." She wrapped her hands around the mug and sipped the tea. The Earl Grey bit her tongue with its strong aftertaste.

"How long will you be staying?" Mom grabbed a sponge and wiped the table down.

"I don't know."

"Two or three days is fine. He'll be at work most of the time. It can be just us girls. Maybe Petra can drive in for the day too. Wouldn't that be fun? We could go shopping. I'll drive us into New Hope to see this new dress shop."

Her mother would not be driving her or anyone any longer. Petra had to take her keys away because their father could not do it. Mom had driven sixty miles away from home before she pulled over on the side of the Garden State Parkway. A state trooper had stopped and helped her.

"What if I wanted to stay longer?" Just long enough to get the house in shape and bring in someone to help around here.

"Let me talk to your father." Her mother patted her hand.

"It's not his decision."

"You don't understand him."

"That's what you always say." It was what her mother had said when she was a teenager and came home after curfew. Or when she brought home a boy that her father didn't approve of and had embarrassed her by saying so in front of the boy. Or when she got a *B* in a class instead of an *A*. Or when her clothes were wrinkled for church. Or any number of things that had happened, making her father angry without reason.

"I have to make lunch." Mom started pulling food from the refrigerator.

"Mom, it's after dinner." She took her mother's hand

and led her back to the table. Mom stared at her with a glassy expression. "I'm sorry if I upset you. Let's finish our tea." Stress made her mother's symptoms worse. She didn't want to upset her mom.

"And that's why you can't stay here," her father said from the doorway. He had been listening. He moved around like a stealthy cat which was why she hadn't heard him come back out.

"I didn't do it on purpose." She hopefully shot a glare at her dad.

"That doesn't matter. You can't come here and start stirring things up. You don't know what's been going on. You're busy with your fancy life." He waved his hand through the air, dismissing her.

Here we go. He would tear her life apart and then complain that she never came around. And when she had lived here, he complained that she was under foot and needed to get out and make a life for herself or find a husband to support her.

"Petra told me everything that's going on here." Petra had asked her to stay put, not to go running home, but she needed to see for herself.

"Petra was wrong. She's a worrier. She doesn't know what she's seeing. I wish I had had sons like my brothers. Sons don't overreact to every little thing."

"Well, if it makes you feel any better, I wish I had a dad who was like my uncles." She grabbed her things off the laundry machines and her suitcase and stormed through the front door.

She couldn't stay here. Who had she been kidding? And she couldn't leave her mother. She would need to find a place to crash, that was all. She had heard her cousin Lacey had opened the bed and breakfast again. But the idea of living on the orchard was just too much. She couldn't bear the idea her father was only an acre or two away.

She understood why none of her extended family had stepped in to help her mom. Huck made that impossible for everyone.

She didn't want to be underfoot at the bed and breakfast and too close to prying eyes. Her cousins would ask too many questions or shake their heads as if they understood what a burden having Huck for a father was and probably silently saying a prayer of thanks they had been born to one of the other Wilde brothers.

Her options were few, but she would be damned if she allowed Huck to send her away. She had learned something from him. She had learned to dig her heels in when she knew she was right.

And she was.

CHAPTER FOUR

Raf slammed the book shut. He couldn't sit still and paced from room to room, looking for answers he didn't have. His brother ruined everything, and he didn't understand why.

His phone vibrated in his pocket. He debated on looking to see who was calling. It could be Tino calling from next door. If it was, let him wait. Voicemail could pick it up, and he could deal with the caller later. When the phone quieted down, he breathed a huge sigh.

Maybe food would get his mind off his problems. In the kitchen, he dumped soup from a can into a pot and turned the flame to low. His phone vibrated again. Whoever it was seemed determined. He dug his phone out of his pocket.

His brother Axel's name lit up the screen. At least it wasn't Tino. "What's up, Ax?"

"Hey, Raf. I'm just checking in. How's it going?" The call sounded as if it were coming from a long tunnel.

"Are you in the car?" Raf stirred his soup and grabbed some bread, sticking it in the toaster oven.

"Yeah. I'm heading back to Candlewood Falls."

"Were you away?" He liked to know when his brothers went away just in case something came up. He even wanted Matias to tell him about his trips and Matt didn't even live in town anymore.

Ax lived in town though, in a small house that needed updating, but on the outskirts where he had lots of property and a space for his artwork. Ax kept to himself, mostly. The third youngest, Ax learned how to fly under the radar. He figured Tino created enough trouble for all four of them. If Ax stayed quiet and did his own thing, no one would pay much attention to him. Which basically worked until he got in trouble for spraying graffiti all over every flat surface he could reach as a kid.

"I was gone just for the day. There's something I need to talk to you about. Can I come by?"

"Now?" Not that he didn't want to see his brother, but he wanted to be alone for the rest of the night after the day he had. He wasn't ready for another brother in need of something. He never felt like he missed out on having kids because of his brothers always coming to him as if he were their dad. And he practically had been. He wasn't complaining, but dealing with Tino today had worn him out.

"Please. It's important. I want to get your opinion on something."

"Okay. I'm heating up some soup if you haven't eaten." He grabbed an extra bowl.

"Soup? Dude, you've got to eat better than that. I'll grab a pizza on my way. Give me twenty. See ya." Ax ended the call before he could point out that pizza was probably a worse food choice than soup.

The idea of eating the soup suddenly didn't appeal to him. He turned off the burner and dumped the soup in a plastic container. Another night he might have called over to Tino to join him, but right now he couldn't even look at his brother. After Ax's visit tonight, he would start looking for therapists in a twenty-mile radius. Tino was going to get his act together if it killed Raf. And it might.

Raf changed out of his work clothes and dragged on an old pair of sweats and a t-shirt that had seen better days. He splashed some cold water on his face and tried to shake the day's events away.

He stole a glance out the window. The rain had let up. Ember Wilde walking away from him as the rain began to fall snuck into his thoughts for the second time today. She was beautiful with that light-brown hair and those bright-blue eyes. She had a full bottom lip he might like to get a taste of if she were any other woman.

Too bad the women who sparked a little interest in him were always off-limits. He could never allow anything other than thoughts to happen with Ember. Not after the humiliation of today, and not with Huck as her father.

Still, he hoped she got home okay. He could ask Brad for her number, just to shoot a quick text, but he had promised not to tell anyone she was here. If for some reason she had changed her mind about going home, he didn't want to blow her cover.

The front door flew open, blasting thoughts of Ember

away and bringing a gust of damp air along with his brother carrying a pizza box.

"Dinner is served." Ax waved a hand over the box and bent his hips in a low bow.

"Thanks. Smells great." The kitchen filled with enticing scents of melted cheese, sauce, and basil. He reached for the cabinet that held the dishes.

"Let me get the plates. Sit down." Ax pushed him toward the chair, but he didn't budge.

"What gives?" His brother wanting to set the table and bring dinner meant something was up Ax's sleeve.

"I don't know what you're talking about." Ax glided past him and grabbed two dishes and two glasses, but avoided any eye contact.

"Axel Alvarez, you have that look on your face like you did that time you brought your girlfriend home late from a date and the dad chased you all the way to our house. You had left my car in their driveway and knew you needed to tell me, but you waited until ten minutes before I had to leave for work in the morning."

"Will you ever get over that?" Ax grabbed slices of pizza, the cheese oozing off the sides in long strings, and put them on each plate. His mouth watered. He didn't realize how hungry he was.

"Nope. Tell me what's on your mind before I eat. I don't want to get an upset stomach." He pulled out the chair, the legs scraping against the tile floor, and he plopped down. He needed to sit for this.

"Fine." Ax took the seat opposite him and ripped a big piece of the slice off with his teeth. "I found something. Well, it's really a someone. And I'm not sure what to do about it." His words tossed around the food in his mouth like clothes stuffed in the dryer.

"Could you not talk while you chomp on your food? Didn't I teach you anything?" Even when their father lived with them, Raf had been the one to help his brothers with life lessons like how to chew with their mouths closed or that homework was important.

"You taught me plenty, Raf. That's why I'm here asking you and not Matt and definitely not Tino about what to do. Your opinion is most important to me. I want your approval." Ax wiped his hands with a napkin.

He leaned back in the chair, leaving the pizza untouched. "Does this have to do with your work?"

"Not exactly. But before I forget, you're still coming to the unveiling, right?"

"I told you I would be there even if it wasn't a guy's night out to celebrate Dax's return." Their high school friend, Dax Fabion, was the town's sports superstar and he was hanging up his professional hockey stick and coming home. The town had commissioned Ax to paint a mural on the outskirts of town across the side of an old building on an abandoned grain farm. There would be an official ceremony, but Ax wanted his friends to see it first.

"You know I get nervous at the opening of any show if you're not there."

Such simple words shouldn't have the ability to fill his chest and steal his breath, but they did. The love he had for his brothers often snuck in and stole his breath like a strong winter wind. "What is it that you wanted to ask me about?" He jumped up and grabbed two beers, giving one to Ax. He popped the top and took a long swig.

"Sit. I'm not sure you're going to like what I have to say, and if you're in the chair, it might be harder for you to hit me when I tell you."

The beer turned to icy dread in his stomach. He took the chair because he didn't have the energy to handle whatever Ax was about to throw at him while standing up. Maybe he had gotten a woman pregnant, which would be fine since Ax was pushing forty himself. They weren't kids. Unless Ax had gambled his money away or gotten addicted to painkillers. "Just say it."

"I found Dad."

The beer slipped from his hand and tumbled to the ground. The glass didn't break, but his sweatpants were covered in cold sticky liquid. What hadn't landed in his lap left a puddle on the floor by his feet.

"Axel, please tell me this is a joke." A joke that wasn't the least bit funny.

"I'm not joking. Actually, he found me. It's a long story, and I can tell you all of it when you calm down." Ax grabbed some paper towels and handed them over.

"I'm calm." He crumpled the paper in his tight fists.

"Um, not by the angry glare in your eyes. Or the fact you haven't moved to clean up the beer you spilled." Ax raised a brow.

He jumped up again and grabbed a dish towel instead, dropping it over the spill on the floor. His pants were toast. He'd need another shower. "See, I'm calm." His racing heart said otherwise, but he wanted to hear the rest of what Ax had to say. He sat back down.

"You're trying hard not to blow your top. I know this

announcement is out of the blue and you have every right to be pissed at Dad and at me for keeping this from you, but you have to know."

"Keeping this from me? How long ago did he find you?" He had worried this time would come. Every year that went by, he hoped they had dodged a bullet, that Johnny would realize they were better off without him, but the time had come like the end of a ticking time bomb.

"Two months."

"What?" He launched out of the chair, knocking it over.

Ax pushed out of the chair too. "Raf, relax. He somehow figured out I was in the street art world and started following me. Anyway, we've been talking. He's changed."

"Yeah, right. He's telling you what you want to hear so he can scam you somehow." That had to be the reason. Ax was the most successful of the four of them, at least when it came to money. It stood to reason Johnny would hit up the son who had the most capital so he could wrap his sweaty fist around it.

"That's not it. Listen for a second." Ax held his hands up in surrender.

"I don't want to listen to any more of this. I have a feeling I know where you're going and it's a hard no."

"He wants to apologize. He wants to make amends with all of us. He's different. He's been in rehab. He's been sober for a long time now. Please, Raf, for me. Just talk to him."

"Don't do this to me. Don't ask me like I'm helping you out of a jam because you know I'd do anything for you. Don't play me, Axel. I won't talk to him ever." No amount of apologizing would be enough. He had been a kid when he realized his father wasn't coming home, and if he hadn't stepped up to the plate, his brothers would have ended up in the system. Tino had been six then.

"You're going to have to at some point. He's coming back to town."

The room turned on its head. He gripped the counter to keep himself from falling to the floor. His phone vibrated next to him like some kind of salvation. He didn't care who was calling. He would talk to anyone to make this crazy conversation stop.

He didn't recognize the number, but he answered anyway. Ax glared at him, probably frustrated that the conversation was interrupted.

"Hello?"

"Hi. Is this Rafael?" A female's soft voice floated over the line. In all likelihood, some telemarketer who had taken acting classes and had a perfect telephone voice.

"Who's asking?"

"This is Ember Wilde. Rafael, is that you?"

Ember Wilde? Now? He couldn't have asked for a better interruption. "How did you get my number?"

"I asked my cousin Brooklyn. She said you wouldn't mind me calling. I hope it's okay."

"Yeah, sure. What can I help you with?" It seemed he was helping everyone today. Everyone but himself. Ax shot him a questioning look. He could only shrug in response.

"I was wondering if that ride you offered was still on the table?"

"You need a ride?" Was he a taxi service now? He

berated himself for the thought. He had offered her a ride earlier, but wasn't there anyone else she could ask for a ride? Like Brooklyn who gave out his number?

"It appears that way. I know I could call a car service, but everyone is thirty or more minutes out. Brooklyn wasn't home when I spoke to her; otherwise, she would do it."

That cleared up the Brooklyn thing.

"Where are you?"

"I'm still at my parents'. I can't stay here and it's too dark to walk back to the train station. I can pay you for the inconvenience."

His life made no sense at the moment. He should tell her no, that he was in the middle of a family crisis, but he had no interest in discussing his father any further with his brother. "You don't have to pay me. Give me five minutes to change." He couldn't show up stinking like a brewery.

"Do you need me to give you the address?"

"I know where it is. I'll be there in fifteen." He ended the call.

"Go home, Ax. This conversation is over. I'm not talking to Dad." He shoved past his brother and ran to change.

Ember Wilde had called him. The first bright spot in the dark and dreary day.

CHAPTER FIVE

E mber checked her phone. Ten minutes had passed since she'd spoken with Rafael. If he didn't arrive soon, she'd have little choice but to walk back to the train station.

She didn't want to be on the porch and have her father find her hanging around. She shouldn't be surprised that he hadn't followed her out, but the sting was still there. No matter how old she got, she wanted her father to at least notice her. Loving her was too much to ask for at this point, but not wanting her to walk away in the dark would be nice.

She dragged her suitcase that bumped and twisted behind her. She would wait by the road so her dad wouldn't pass by a window and accidently see her. The darkness swallowed up the end of the driveway, making it nearly impossible to see her hand in front of her face. The street was absent of lights and the other houses were too far from the road for the glow from their windows to do much good. She would not think about the serial killer podcasts she listened to.

A speck of light formed at the end of the street and grew into two perfect circles as it drew closer. The roar of an engine, something old and without a muffler, followed on the heels of the light, now clearly fully formed headlights.

The truck slowed as it approached her. She gripped her phone in her pocket. Rafael stuck his head out the window. She let out a long breath.

"You really were waiting outside. You can toss your bag in the back." He hitched a thumb over his shoulder to the flatbed, but didn't get out of the truck.

She heaved her bag, almost dropping it into the back with a thud. She was an independent woman who didn't need a man's help, but after the day she had, a little male muscle would have been nice. But what did she expect? She had made herself clear to him earlier. Maybe she'd learn to keep her mouth shut once in a while.

"You're still out here." Her father appeared like an apparition at the end of the driveway, taking a few years off her life.

"Dad, you scared me. What are you doing out here?" Had he come after all to make sure she was okay?

"Taking out the garbage. I saw the vehicle and some movement. I came to check what was happening near my property. Didn't want some misbehaving teenagers digging anything up."

"Hello, Huck," Rafael said.

Dad's head swung around as if he just realized a truck was actually idling in the road. "Alvarez, what are you doing here? Hasn't your family caused enough prob-lems for one day?"

She didn't know what that meant and wasn't going to ask. It must have something to do with the orchard, which was none of her business.

"It's nice to see you too." The sarcasm dripped off Rafael's words like cooking grease.

"He's my ride." She held her father's gaze.

"Of course, you're getting in the truck with him. You never cared much for what other people think."

Her father's narrow mind was giving her a migraine behind her eyes. "It's a ride, Dad. Why do you care anyway? You didn't want me in the house, and now you don't like the way I'm leaving."

"I don't want you hanging around with him." Her father jabbed a finger at Rafael.

Rafael jumped from the truck and stood inches from her father. "I don't care what you think about me, but when I'm standing right in front of you, keep it to yourself."

Her father backed up and threw a hand in the air. "Suit yourself, Ember Rose." He lumbered up the driveway without a look back. He didn't have the garbage can with him.

"I'm so sorry, Rafael." Her heart palpitated against her ribs. She forced air into her lungs to calm down.

"Call me Raf. And don't be sorry." He wiped a hand over his face. "Huck and I usually go at it a couple of times a month. He doesn't like me because I'm Spanish, because of my background, and because he's forced to listen to me at work." He slid into the driver's seat.

She hurried around the truck and slid in beside him.

The truck was neat and smelled of aftershave lotion. She couldn't defend her father just because he was difficult on the best days. She didn't doubt Raf's assessment, but hearing it still weighed heavy on her. "Is he going to give you a bad time tomorrow at the orchard because you helped me out?"

Raf turned the truck around and went back the way he had come. "I can handle him. Where can I take you?"

"The train station." She would go back to the apartment in the city and ask Keith if she could stay there a little longer, just until she found another place to live. And then she would figure out a way to help her mother remotely.

She could stop in during the days when her father was at work. She might even be able to arrange for a healthcare worker to come in from time to time or a cleaning person at least.

"The train doesn't run at night." Raf gave her a sideways glance.

"It doesn't?" She had forgotten in all the stress of dealing with her father and witnessing her mother with that empty look in her eyes.

"I guess you've forgotten Candlewood Falls is a small town. The train keeps a commuter schedule only." A small smile tilted his lips.

She would need a place to sleep for the night, and then she could catch the train in the morning. Which made no sense now because by the time she got to the apartment she would have to turn around and come back. "Do you know of any hotels?"

Raf's phone rang inside the truck before he could

answer her question. The name of the caller, Ax, popped up on the screen in his dashboard.

Raf hit the decline button. "Oh no. Not now."

"Guess you don't want to talk to him. Assuming it's a him." She could relate to the feeling of wanting to be left alone.

"He's my brother Axel. Do you remember him?" Raf turned at the stop sign.

She racked her brain for a memory and could pull a tiny sliver of a young man who walked around the high school with his flannel shirts unbuttoned, revealing his chest in all its glory. His long black hair bounced off his shoulders when he walked. "Was he the one who didn't seem to know how to button his shirts?"

Raf barked out a laugh. "You remember that?"

"I do, strangely enough." Because that young man had been wild and dangerous compared to her. And honestly, sexy in that bad boy way. Huck watched her every move like a hawk. If she so much as put a toe out of line, her father brought his anger down on her.

"That was me."

Heat flushed her cheeks. She slapped her hands over her face, grateful he couldn't read her thoughts.

"Ax was usually covered in paint." He shook his head and smirked.

"Got it." Did she ever. Raf had snagged her attention when she didn't even know she had been looking.

"How about the bed and breakfast on the orchard?" He hit his turn signal and made a right onto another dark and winding road.

"No. I don't want to see any family."

"I can understand that." He stopped the truck and turned around. "I'll go in another direction then."

The phone rang again. Raf hit the decline button on Ax for the second time.

"Maybe it's important." She couldn't imagine ignoring a call from Petra or Nyx, no matter what was happening in her life at that moment.

"I don't want to talk to him right now. I can drive you over to Clinton. They have a Marriott. Would that work?"

"A Marriott is fine. Thank you very much for coming to get me. I should have said that sooner. I really do appreciate it. My father was being difficult, and I panicked and ran." Like she always did when it came to her father, the faster she got away the better.

"You don't have to explain to me." He took the exit on the left for Route 78.

The phone rang again. Raf reached for the button, but her hand gripped his wrist. "I'm sure it's none of my business, but if my sisters tried me three times in a row, I would answer. It might be an emergency."

He gave her a quick glance and hit the accept button. "Axel, this better be important."

"Raf, it's about Tino. Something happened." Ax's voice filled the truck.

"I don't care." The muscle in Raf's jaw twitched.

"No, listen. He's gone."

"Gone where? Out to Murphy's?"

Murphy's had been the one bar in town. Looked as if it still was. Good to see the people of Candlewood Falls hadn't given up their nighttime escapes. Maybe that's where she should have Raf drop her instead of the Marriott.

"I don't know where he went. I stopped by his place after yours. The door was unlocked, but he wasn't inside. His clothes are gone, and the keys to the house are on the kitchen table. I tried calling him, but he doesn't answer. It goes right to voicemail."

Raf banged the steering wheel. "You know what, I really don't care. If he wants to run away, then let him. He's caused me enough trouble."

"You should come home right away," Ax said.

"I'm busy right now."

"He left a note. And Raf... he trashed the place."

"I'll be right there." Raf ended the call and turned to her. "I'm sorry. Would you mind if we made a quick stop at my house? My brother Tino rents one half of the house from me. I have to see what he's done. Then I can drop you or you can wait for the ride service from my place."

"Sure. Of course. I don't have anywhere to be." Or anyone waiting for her.

Raf stood in the kitchen of Tino's half of the house and turned in circles. His boots stuck to the floor or crunched over something as he stepped on it.

He couldn't believe his eyes or the sour smell. Tino had dumped every ounce of food on the floor. All the sugar, the flour, the pickles and their juices, the eggs, the milk, the cereal. He had dumped the garbage can which had been full and as rancid as fertilizer.

In the bathroom, Tino had squirted the shampoo and conditioner until it covered the floor and the shower. He had sprayed shaving cream all over the counter and the sink. He had cut all the bedsheets to shreds. He had punched a couple of holes in the bedroom wall.

Tino had ravaged the apartment like a tornado coming through town. He had sliced gaping holes into the sofa cushions and pulled out all the stuffing. For whatever reason, he hadn't smashed the television or broken any of the glass or mirrors. He probably didn't want to be found out until he was long gone. Breaking things would have tipped Raf off that something was going on, since the houses were attached.

Ax huddled in the corner with his hands in his pockets and a despondent look on his face. At least Ember was waiting next door at his place. He hadn't wanted her to see whatever it was Tino had done. Having a brother like Tino was sometimes embarrassing. And he didn't want her to think for a second that he or even Ax was like Tino.

"It's not your fault, Ax." He picked his way through the food and kicked off his boots so as not to track more of a mess into the living room. At least in here it was only Dacron and fabric scattered all over. Being the brother born right before Tino, Ax often felt responsible for him, but Tino never regarded Ax with much respect. Tino didn't respect anyone or anything, actually.

"I know it's not, but I wish I knew what was going through Tino's mind. Why would he do this to you?"

"He's pissed off because he got caught stealing at the orchard today." And because Tino thought the world owed him. Even though they had been dealt a bad hand in the parent area, no one owed Tino a thing. He just hadn't gotten on board with that idea.

"What did Brad do when that happened?" Ax's mouth gaped open.

"I begged Brad not to send him to jail. I might have been wrong about that one." He should have allowed Brad to throw Tino's ass behind bars. Tino needed to learn his lesson and losing his freedom might be the only way to get through to him. But still, the idea of Tino in prison sent an icy dread down his back. He couldn't allow Tino to end up like that. He would have no chance at a life. At least out here, Raf could keep an eye on him, and maybe, in time, Tino would come around.

"I'll help you clean this up."

"No, go home. I'll call someone in to do it." He knew a pretty good cleaning service, and he couldn't stomach doing it himself. Not tonight anyway. "And, Ax, please don't tell Johnny about this, okay?"

"Yeah, sure. If that's what you want."

"It's what I want. I don't want him knowing anything about Tino and what he's like."

"He's Tino's dad too. Maybe he can help."

"You really think so, huh? It's his damn fault that Tino is the way he is in the first place. He wasn't around for any of us when Mom was busy shooting up. He didn't give a damn about his sons when we needed him. Instead, he disappeared, almost separating us permanently. If I hadn't been eighteen, we would have been. I don't care what kind of bullshit he's thrown at you. He's a liar. So, just do me the one favor and don't say a word to him about any of this."

"Okay, okay. I won't say anything." Ax held his

hands in the air. "If you change your mind about the cleanup help, call me."

He patted Ax on the shoulder. "I can handle this." He waited until Ax's car backed out of the driveway, then pulled his phone out and pulled up Brad's number from his favorites list.

"Hey," Brad said on the second ring.

"Hey, man. I'm sorry to ask for a favor after today, but is there anyway Lyra can send a cleaning crew over to my house?" Brad's girlfriend, Lyra, had started a cleaning business last November. She made a point to employ women who were trying to get on their feet after being in a bad relationship because that was why she had begun cleaning herself. In her spare time, she ran a group therapy session too.

"Right now?" Brad's voice tilted with surprise.

"Now."

"What happened?"

He took a deep breath and dove into the story, leaving out all the parts about his father returning to Candlewood Falls. He just couldn't handle that conversation on top of everything else. "Please don't say you told me so."

"Not me. But your brother is a real pain in the ass. Hold on. I'll get Lyra. She's in the other room with the kids." Brad moved the phone around as if he was putting it down and called to Lyra somewhere in their house.

A few minutes later, Lyra grabbed the phone. "Hi, Raf. Brad told me everything. Are you okay?"

"I'm fine. Is it too late to get some of your people here? If I have to wait until tomorrow, I understand, but it stinks with the garbage and the food everywhere."

"Don't worry. I've already sent a text to Vaughn. His group will be there in thirty minutes. If you don't want to wait, leave the door unlocked."

"Thank you. Just send me the bill when it's done." He would add this expense to Tino's tab.

"I don't charge family. If you need anything else, just let me know. Good night, Raf. And good luck. It sounds like you might need it."

He sure did.

CHAPTER SIX

Ember's hand hovered above the doorknob. She wanted to go next door and help Raf. He hadn't been able to cover up the pain crossing his face before she noticed. Whatever his brother had done couldn't be good. But Raf had asked her to stay in his house. She should honor that, but he shouldn't be there alone.

She gripped the knob and opened the door, stepping out onto the porch. The rain had started up again. A chill ran over her skin. The door to the other house swung open and a man came out, stopping short when he noticed her. He was similar in appearance and size to Raf. This was Ax.

"Who are you?" he said, narrowing his eyes. "Wait a second. You're Ember Wilde. Your younger sister is Nicole."

"That's right. Hi, Ax." Everyone knew Nyx. She had been Miss Popularity in high school. She had starred in the musical and won best band three years in a row at the high school's Battle of the Bands. "I wanted to come inside and help."

"Help with what?"

"I was in the truck when you called. I know something is wrong in there. He shouldn't be left alone to deal with it." Her sisters would never hightail it out on her in a crisis. They always had each other's backs. That was the one good thing about having Huck for a father. It had brought her closer to her sisters. They had no one else to rely on but each other.

Ax had the decency to look slightly embarrassed. "I wouldn't go in there if I were you. He's pretty pissed off."

"So, you leave him? What kind of a brother are you?" She slammed her mouth shut, but words were slippery creatures and long gone.

"Are you two dating or something? I'm not sure why else you'd be all up in my business." Embarrassment quickly dissipated into snarky sarcasm.

She took a calming breath, giving her time to think. The need to protect Raf from whatever he was dealing with had overwhelmed her. She couldn't figure out why —maybe it was because she had needed a little protection today—but whatever the reason, he was a nice guy.

"We're friends." That was a bit of a stretch. They had just reconnected today. If it could even be called reconnecting. It wasn't as if they were friends growing up.

"Ember, take my advice and stay out of this."

"I don't think I can do that." *Oh, that mouth of hers.* "He was very upset when we arrived. I just want to help him. Are you going to move away from the door?" She didn't have to be a girlfriend to be concerned about another human, especially one who had been so pleasant to her right from the start.

"If Raf asked you to wait, you should wait. I wish I could stick around to make sure you don't go in there, but I've got other family matters to deal with. Don't say I didn't warn you." He hurried to his car.

She waited only long enough for Ax to pull away before opening the door and sticking her head in. "Raf? Do you need any help?"

The door opened into a small hallway with a living room off to the left and a staircase immediately in front of her. The hallway led back to a kitchen. A few cabinet doors hung open, revealing empty cabinets. Something was all over the floor.

"Ember, stay out there." Raf ran down the steps two at a time.

"What happened?" She inched in a little more.

"Never mind. I have it under control." He put a hand on her shoulder and turned her back toward the porch.

"You were gone a while. I thought you could use some help with whatever happened. What did happen?" She planted her feet and turned back, holding his gaze.

"Nothing I can't handle, but thank you for caring." He made a turning motion with his finger.

"You're a stubborn one." If the man needed to hang on to his pride, she could give him that much. He wasn't throwing it around like an ape at least.

"Blame it on my Spanish heritage."

"Something tells me your heritage has nothing to do with it." She would, however, give his heritage plenty of credit for his dark good looks.

Headlights turned into the driveway and bounced

closer to the house, stopping behind Raf's truck. This place was like a hotel with all the people coming and going. She would need to call that ride service after all. He wasn't going to be able to take her, and she wanted to put her feet up and close her eyes. The day had worn her out. If she couldn't be of any service to him, she might as well get on with her life and let him get on with his.

Three people jumped out of a dark sedan. She couldn't make out the model, but two women and a man grabbed things from the trunk and hurried toward the porch. Maybe a cleaning crew from the looks of the garbage bags and the mops they carried.

"Go inside. I'll be right there." Raf opened the door to his side of the house and waited for her to pass him.

"Look, I'm just going to call for a ride. You've got enough to deal with." And she had problems of her own to resolve.

"Give me five minutes. I'll drive you. I promise."

"It's okay, Raf. You don't owe me anything." She wasn't used to anyone trying so hard to help her. Most of the time, when it wasn't one of her sisters, she had to rely on herself to meet her needs.

"Raf Alvarez? I'm Vaughn King," the man carrying the mop said. "I work for Lyra. She said you had an emergency."

Raf looked at her, then back at Vaughn.

"I'll wait inside." She closed the door behind her. Whatever Tino did, he had made a mess and probably a big one. Hopefully, it didn't involve bodily fluids.

The sofa, a tan sectional taking up most of the living room, invited her to sink into it with its oversized pillows. The hardwood floors and shaggy area rug warmed the room. The coffee table was distressed as if someone had created it by hand. The fireplace was surrounded by stone. Maybe an original part of the house.

The sofa's material was soft under her fingers. She left trails in the fabric from where she touched it. A blanket was folded on the corner. This was probably a favorite napping spot. She kicked off her shoes and grabbed the blanket. Tucking herself into the corner of the sectional, she wrapped the blanket around her. It smelled peppery and spicy, very male. She snuggled into the cushions.

"I'm back." Raf's voice was in the room before he was.

"That was quick," she said from her spot on the sofa. Raf had said to make herself at home. She could have used about ten minutes with her eyes closed before he returned. So, she kept them closed now.

"I can take you to the hotel." The cushion beside her sunk under his weight. She caught a whiff of that spicy male scent that was also on the blanket.

She propped open one eye and found him looking at her. Dark half-moons hung under his bloodshot eyes. "Do you want to talk about it?" She pushed herself into a sitting position and tossed the blanket aside.

"Not really."

"You might feel better." Raf seemed like a decent guy who was shafted by his brother and could use a little comfort.

"It's a long story, and I'm too tired to drag it all out." He leaned his head back on the cushions and closed his eyes.

"How about a beer? Do you have any?" If she were being honest with herself, the last thing she wanted to do was spend the night alone in a hotel room, replaying the entire conversation with her father until her blood boiled over. She wasn't in a hurry to get anywhere. If Raf needed a few minutes, she would be happy to wait.

She had spent plenty of nights alone even when she was married to Keith. The marriage certificate had her name on it, but he was really married to his job. She didn't like hers anywhere near enough to put in the time and attention that he did. Maybe if she had followed her heart instead of her father's demand for a sensible career, at least she'd have a job she could lean on.

"Beer's in the fridge." He pointed in the general direction of the kitchen.

She hopped off the couch, careful not to trip over his long legs, but she did steal a second look since his eyes were closed. Oh yeah, Rafael Alvarez and his strong, beard-dusted jaw was worth a second glance.

She returned with two bottles and tapped his shoulder with one.

"Thanks," he said with a half smile. "So, tell me why you're in town."

"I came to visit my mother." She didn't want to explain the rest. They had the *let's not talk about our crazy families* in common.

"Let me guess. Things with Huck went badly and that's why you called me for a ride." He eyed her over the bottle.

"How about we table all difficult topics of discussion for the time being?" She took a sip of the beer and waited for the moment when her shoulders dropped down out of her ears, but that didn't happen.

She would need more than one sip to smooth the rough edges of her father's behavior from her mind. She might even need a full bottle before she could figure out how to handle him and her mother's condition. She would be calling Petra in the morning for some advice.

"Fair enough." He held his bottle up to hers. She clinked them together, but he didn't drink. "I should get you to that hotel. I said I would drive you, and I'm a man of my word."

She didn't doubt that. "Would I be out of line if I said you looked a little tired?"

"I'm beat, actually." He wiped a hand over his face.

"Would it be easier if you didn't have to drive me?" An idea formed in her mind. She should ignore it, pretend it wasn't there, but it was quickly becoming like a scab she couldn't stay away from.

"Then how will you get there?"

"Your couch seems pretty comfy." The night had dragged on. He was clearly too tired to drive. Even if he was a bit chauvinistic, the least she could do was give a guy a break after the day he had.

"You want to sleep on my couch?" The surprise in his voice rang throughout the room.

"If it's all right with you. You can always drop me in the morning when you're rested. Besides, driving while tired is worse than driving drunk. I heard that some-where. Unless of course, you would rather I not sleep here. Which I understand too." Her words tumbled out of her mouth. So what if she made hasty decisions. They didn't all have to be bad. Why should sleeping at Raf's have to be?

He choked out a tired laugh. "You are more than welcome to my couch. In fact, I appreciate you thinking of me. Not too many people do that these days. I have another blanket in the closet by the door. But if you decide you want a bed, it's the second door on the left. Good night, Ember."

"Good night." She waited for the sound of a door closing, then jumped up and grabbed her phone. Her fingers flew across the screen until she had Petra's number ringing.

"Ember?" Petra's sleep-clogged voice came across the line. "Why are you calling so late?"

"Dad threw me out of the house."

"You went home?" Petra's voice was suddenly clear. She lived alone, except for her daughter, but she was away at college. Petra was wrapping up her divorce. There hadn't been any worry of waking up a companion.

She hadn't bothered to tell her sister her plan to high-tail it out of the city and make a surprise return to their childhood home. She hadn't told her because she hadn't bothered to plan a thing.

"After your call, I had to see Mom. She seems fine now. Not like you said at all."

"I'm sure she was, but it doesn't last. Where are you? Are you back at your place?" Petra let out a loud yawn.

"I gave Keith the apartment." She drank more of the beer and picked at the fuzz on her pants.

"Are you crazy? That's a beautiful apartment."

"I hated it." She glanced around Raf's living room. This was the kind of home she had always wanted.

Something not too big, but warm and homey. Something with a yard on a quiet street. "I'm back in Candlewood Falls and staying at a… a friend's house."

"A friend? Do you still have friends in Candlewood Falls?"

"Is that supposed to be a joke?" She finished off the beer and wrapped the blanket around her.

"Just tell me. I need some good gossip. My life revolves around ending my marriage and selling my house."

"I'm spending the night at Raf Alvarez's house. Do you remember him?" Before today she hadn't given Raf Alvarez a second thought. And that memory of him walking the halls without his shirt unbuttoned was like finding a ten-dollar bill in a coat not worn in years.

"Should I?"

"He was in my grade. Tall. Dark. Very handsome."

"Sorry. Name sounds familiar but I can't place him. Wait a second. Did you sleep with him?" Petra's voice was filled with shock and horror. "Please tell me you didn't jump into bed with him right away."

"What? No. Uh, Petra, you have a dirty mind."

"Then why are you there?" Petra dropped her voice into a stage whisper as if Raf could hear her.

She tried not to laugh. "It's a long story, but I'm crashing on his couch for the night. I just wanted someone to know." Just in case she was completely wrong about him.

"He didn't give up his bed? What kind of a man is he?"

"I offered to sleep on the couch. He doesn't have to give up his bed." Petra was born in the wrong decade.

She expected a man to open a door for her or give up his seat on the subway.

"He would if he were a real man."

"Oh, he's real all right. And thinks a lot like you. Anyway, I'm going back tomorrow to spend more time with Mom. I'll keep you posted." This time she would make sure her father wasn't home.

"Ember, I think it's great that you want to help out Mom, but trust me. You're wasting your time. Go home."

She didn't have a home, but she did have time. "I'll call you tomorrow. Go back to sleep. Love you madly."

"Love you more."

CHAPTER SEVEN

Raf closed his laptop and tossed his glasses on the bed. His eyes were as dry as dust. He had left Ember downstairs about two hours ago, saying he wanted to sleep. But he couldn't sleep, not with what Tino had done to the house.

His brother had taken the old cans of paint in the basement and painted black lines all over the bedrooms, making sure to get some of the furniture too. He had also managed to put glue in the backdoor lock which would now need to be replaced. Tino had moved with lightning speed to complete his destruction and get away. His brother was good at causing trouble, and he was dumb enough to believe Tino would change.

Raf grabbed his phone on the side table and brought up Tino's number. He wasn't surprised the call went straight to voicemail. Tino probably hadn't paid his phone bill.

"How could you do this to me? After everything I've done for you. You repay me from keeping you out of jail by trashing my house? I should've let Brad call the police." He ended the call and tossed the phone back on the table.

The cleaning crew was going to cost him a grand. He had some money in the bank, but he didn't want to drain it all dry, and he didn't want any credit card debt. He couldn't report the vandalism, no matter what he just said on the voicemail, so that meant no going through insurance.

He would also need to get a tenant who could pay rent. That had been the whole point of buying this house in the first place. He could rent out half to make the mortgage easier. With Tino living next door, he had been carrying the full nut and it was costing him.

He threw the covers back and went to the window where the rain smacked against it with an angry force. He could relate. The temperature in the room had dropped, turning the hardwood to ice, even in April. The winter temperatures were making a last-ditch effort to hang on.

He shivered but didn't move. The cold kept him alert and he wanted to figure out what he was going to do next. Did he look for Tino? Or did he give up on his brother? And if he found him, what did he expect?

The door creaked on its hinges, startling him. The light in the hallway backlit Ember stumbling into the room. Had she too much to drink or simply didn't know where she was going in the dark?

"Are you okay?" he said.

She screamed like a hyena. "Oh my God. You scared me. I thought you said this was the guest room."

"Sorry. Didn't mean to frighten you." He bit back a

laugh. "You fell through the doorway. I thought maybe you stepped on your shoelace or something. The guest room is the next door down, by the way." He turned his gaze away, but stubborn as it was, his gaze returned to her. He should have checked to see if she needed anything, but his lack of female overnight guests recently had him out of practice.

"It's freezing downstairs. Don't you have any heat in this place?" She rubbed her arms.

"It's broken. The comforter in the other room is made from down. That should help. I also have a sleeping bag." He liked to camp even in the cold. He had all the supplies for a night out in the woods. He doubted Ember would be interested in something like that. She hadn't even arrived in town prepared for the rain.

"How about if you light a fire in that pretty nice fireplace and we sleep down there together?"

"You want to light a fire?" Maybe he was wrong about the camping thing, but her clothes said high-end — ones that probably cost more than his ever would. Each piece fit her like a glove, as if they were made for her. She carried herself with poise too. It was actually hard to picture her as Huck's daughter.

"Didn't I just say that?" She rubbed her arms again and blew on her hands.

"I wasn't going to sleep anyway." That biting remark sounded a lot like her father, but coming from her lips the pain wasn't there.

He followed her back downstairs. She huddled under the blankets while he moved around putting logs on the fire. When the fire took, he sat beside her. The glow from the flames danced up the wall in long shadows. A beautiful woman occupied space on his couch. If he thought about nothing else except Ember and the fire—so like her name—he could forget about his problems.

"You want some?" She held up the edge of the blanket.

"I'm good. Thanks." He wasn't ready to close in on her personal space. It wasn't as if he couldn't control himself, but she smelled sweet and spicy—like cinnamon—and her smile nudged on the shoulder of his slumbering inclinations.

"Did your brother have something to do with the lack of heat?" She stretched out her legs until her feet rested on his thighs. "Do you mind?" She lifted her feet and held them in midair.

He shrugged as if he couldn't care less, but his heart picked up speed. He was attracted to her. He couldn't deny that. And he liked that she felt comfortable with him. She knew what she wanted it seemed and grabbed for it. He admired that trait in her.

"I'm sorry to say Tino is the reason we're without working heat." Lying would serve no purpose, and he didn't think he had to with her. She was Huck's daughter. She had to know what kind of things Huck said and did to others.

"What are you going to do about it?" She wiggled under the blanket more, moving her feet up and down his leg, as she settled into the sofa. He was pretty sure it wasn't a come on. He might be out of practice, but not that much.

"I don't know yet. I don't even know where he went." He couldn't focus on a conversation if she continued to brush against him that way. Their proximity might be doing nothing to her, but he hadn't been intimate with a woman in longer than he cared to admit. All this physical touching was a little more than he could take.

"Family can be difficult." Her words startled his thoughts away.

"We have that in common. Do you want some water?" He eased out from under her and went into the kitchen. She might not need anything to drink, but he sure as hell did. His throat could sand the roughest of woods.

"No, thanks. So, what do you do for fun around here?"

"Fun? What's that?" He swigged a big gulp from the water bottle. "I thought you wanted to sleep."

"I can't now. So, tell me something you like to do."

He dropped into the chair opposite the couch and plopped his feet up on the table. "I have a thing with a few guys on Friday night. Do you remember Dax Fabion?"

"Sure. Big-time hockey player. Went pro."

"He's back in town. Me and a couple of old friends are going to celebrate. Not a big deal. Besides that, I whittle once in a while. What about you? What do you do for fun?" He wanted to know what made her smile or laugh out loud and what kind of things she was drawn to. In all the Tino chaos, she was a breath of fresh air.

"I don't remember." The light from the flames captured the sadness crossing over her eyes. "It's been a long time since I've done anything fun. Except maybe this sleepover." In a flash, her smile chased the darkness away.

"You might need a hobby then. Are you warmer

now?" The heat from the fire dried out his throat more. He downed the last of the water.

"I think so. Thanks for the fire."

"My pleasure. If you're all good, I'm going back to bed." He needed to get some sleep and wouldn't be able to with her in the room. The shadows danced around her, softening her. He would watch all night until the sun came up and pushed the veil away. Then her beauty would be stark and brilliant, and he would never be the same.

She caught his wrist. His gaze dropped to where their skin met and then to the blaze of her blue eyes. "I thought you were going to sleep down here with me."

He wasn't sure if he was reading her correctly. If he was wrong, and made a move, he would make an ass out of himself. He was crazy to think Ember was putting out signals. They barely knew each other, and he wasn't into one-night stands. He doubted she was either. He was just lonely. That was all. "I think it's better if I go upstairs."

"Why?"

"You don't want anything to do with me, Ember. Your father won't approve."

"What does my father have to do with anything?" She pushed off the couch and stood toe to toe with him.

"Huck has an opinion about everything. He will voice his concerns to you about me. They won't be true, but he doesn't always care about that. He only cares about what he believes." He waited to get slapped, but she leaned closer.

"I'm a grown woman who doesn't need her father's approval to kiss a man."

He swallowed hard. What he thought was only

possible innuendo was now crystal clear. He should hustle his ass up those steps and close the door. "You want me to kiss you?"

"I thought you could tell. I'm sorry if I was wrong." She stepped away.

This time he held her wrist and tugged her nearer. Her smile seduced him, giving him the go ahead. He cupped her face and kissed her.

He parted her lips with his tongue. As they tangled together, it was as if the earth opened and sent him tumbling. A jolt shot through him, and his brain was anything but foggy with the need for sleep now.

She wrapped her arms around his neck and placed her hands on the back of his head. She pulled him closer and let out a small moan.

He was in trouble. He wanted to take Huck Wilde's daughter to bed. That would probably get him killed. But would it stop him?

He eased out of the kiss, resting his forehead on hers. "This is where I say good night, Ember."

"Good night, Raf."

CHAPTER EIGHT

E mber opened and closed cabinets in Raf's kitchen. The sun had barely cleared the horizon line, but she couldn't sit still any longer. Sleep had escaped her most of the night. She kept thinking about how good Raf looked in his gym shorts and t-shirt last night. And after he had built that fire, she couldn't look away from the flames dancing in his dark eyes. His gaze had smoldered. Or maybe that had been her. She hadn't come to Candlewood Falls with any thoughts of a man, but in less than twenty-four hours, she had found the hottest guy she had ever seen. Too bad he worked at the orchard and knew her father. And too bad she knew how her father would react to her dating a man named Rafael Alvarez.

Her haste could end up breaking her heart. She hadn't thought about what marrying Keith had meant when they had hopped a plane to Vegas, and she should have. Jumping into bed with Raf might be nice, but it would also cause a tidal wave of problems.

The one good thing no sleep helped her with was

figuring out her next move where her mother was concerned. She needed a place to stay in town, then her father would be powerless to make her go. She could show up at the house while he was at work and spend time with her mother, looking after her. Once she had a good assessment of her mother's condition, she would find the best care. Because Huck Wilde was not it. He didn't care about his wife. He didn't care about much of anything.

Success in the form of a plastic container of coffee in the fridge appeared as she pushed what might be leftovers to the side. The coffee maker was the basic kind with a carafe and basket for the grinds. Guess he wasn't much of a coffee drinker, but she couldn't jumpstart her day without a strong cup.

"Good morning." Raf sauntered into the kitchen. His hair was still wet from a shower. He had a clean-shaven face and had switched his sleepwear for a sweatshirt and jeans. His feet were bare. His good looks set her off-kilter. She gripped the counter for balance.

"Good morning. Hope you don't mind." She held up the mug she had also succeeded in finding.

"Not at all. Hey, about last night…"

"Forget it. It was late. We were both tired from two really bad days." She had told herself that excuse for the better part of the last hour. He could not have meant to kiss her in a seductive *want to kiss you more* kind of way even if she had wanted that. And she had from the moment she had stumbled into his bedroom like a love-struck fool.

She actually hadn't meant to go in there. She really was looking for the guest room. She had hoped it would be warmer upstairs. But it was dark, and she hadn't known how far down the hall she had walked. She opened the first door she came across. Lucky her it had been his.

The pull that charged the air when he was around was tangible. That had been the reason she had called him for the ride, and the reason she had wanted to stick around. She could have easily gone anywhere else. Well, not anywhere.

"I'm glad you said that. I didn't want you to think that I was trying to take advantage of you or anything. It was... well, whatever it was, I shouldn't have kissed you."

She tried to hide the disappointment from her face. She hadn't regretted that kiss at all. His kiss, though short and sweet, had vibrated down to her toes.

"Do you want some coffee?" She didn't know what else to say to him. She couldn't very well tell him to kiss her again. Could she? Instead, she pulled a second mug down from the cabinet and held it out.

"I usually grab mine at the orchard when I get to work. Will you be here later?" He pulled socks out of his back pants pockets and shoved his feet in them.

"Do you want me to be?" She berated herself for sounding like an eager hall monitor.

"You're welcome to stay as long as you like. Grab a shower. Whatever you need," he said over his shoulder as he grabbed his work boots by the door.

She wasn't ready to see him go. "What's going to happen with the other half of your place?"

"I need to rent it out as soon as possible." He gathered his keys and wallet from the table.

"Have you found someone yet?" The idea formed in her head as the words floated from her mouth. She had way crazier ideas than this one.

"Since last night?" He choked out a laugh. "Nope. Do you know someone who needs a place to stay?" He laughed more at his own joke, probably not knowing how close he hit.

"Actually, I do." She put the mug down, straightened her shoulders, and met his gaze head-on.

He stopped laughing and stared at her with a blank face.

"Could I rent it? For a month or so. That's all."

He remained silent.

Her idea started to dissipate as if it were a puffy cloud. "I understand if that doesn't work with your plans... but you'd really be helping me out." She forced her gaze to stay straight on him instead of dropping to her feet like it wanted. What was she thinking, asking this man—a practical stranger—to rent out his apartment to her when only a few hours ago his brother had done so much damage he had to call a cleaning crew to make it right?

"Do you have any references? My last tenant didn't pay any rent and trashed the place." He cocked his head and narrowed his eyes as if scrutinizing his options, but the smile on his lips said something else.

"Are you joking?" She couldn't quite tell.

"Only a little." One side of his lip curled up further. "Why do you want to move next door?"

"Because I need a place to live while I'm in town." She hoped he would spare her the embarrassment of having to say out loud that she wasn't welcomed in her own home.

"Stay with me."

"Wait. You mean here?" Now she was completely confused.

"I don't live anywhere else." That crooked smile straightened out to a full-blown knock her over smile.

"But you have a whole house attached. I can pay the rent, you know." She couldn't dream of sharing space with him. That was too forward—even for her.

He had plenty of room with three bedrooms upstairs. And she was pretty sure there were two full baths upstairs. Living here would be a good way to get back at her father for throwing her out, but the gravitational pull toward Mr. Alvarez was lighting up like an old-time switchboard. She could end up powerless to it. And she had no intention of complicating this visit with a relationship of any kind. Of course, she wasn't thinking that last night when she had wanted to kiss him. She could blame the lack of sleep or the fire or even the beer she had drunk earlier in the evening.

"I don't doubt that you can pay every penny including a security deposit. But I need top dollar for the place. I won't feel right asking for that much from you."

"Why? Because I'm a woman?"

He threw his hands up in the air. "What does you being a woman have to do with anything? Except of course that you're probably the most beautiful woman to step inside my house. I don't want to undercharge you because you're a woman. But because you are a Wilde. And no matter what is going on between me and your extended family, I would not ever—and I mean ever—

take advantage of one of them. But you go ahead and believe my motives are totally chauvinistic. Because every guy must be like your dad, right?"

His words halted the next thing out of her mouth. She was ready to assault him with accusations of thinking she was helpless and dependent on others. But this time he had hit the bullseye. She assessed every man against her father to make sure they were not, in fact, anything like him. "I don't think every man is like my father."

"Okay. You go on believing that. I'll be back later. If you're here when I return, I'll take that as a yes to staying with me. If you're not, then I wish you well, Ember Wilde." He turned and disappeared through the doorway. He was out the front door without another word.

She grabbed her phone and called Petra.

"How's it going?" Petra said after the second ring.

"Raf wants me to live with him." She returned to her quest for a cup of coffee, but her recent banter with Raf had the blood pumping just fine through her veins.

"What? You just bumped into him for the first time in what... twenty some odd years? That's moving pretty fast, don't you think?"

"Not like that. Geez. Like a roommate."

"Okay. I have a ton of questions."

She told Petra the whole story from the minute she entered his bedroom.

"I don't think that's a good idea, Ember. The last thing we need is Dad all up in arms. He's going to be difficult enough to deal with when we tell him we want a say in what happens to Mom. Why aggravate the situation by living with a man you don't know and one whose last name is Alvarez?"

"Dad doesn't get to tell me what to do or who to do it with." That reason alone was enough to accept Raf's offer.

"I know that. No one does. But you being in town is about Mom. Mom needs us. And if I could have gone myself, I would be there even if I had to pitch a tent in the backyard. Just live at the house. It's what's best for everyone."

"What harm would it do?" She wanted to stay. She couldn't deny it, no matter the reason.

"Probably a lot. Hey, I need to let you go. The septic guy is here. Talk soon. But go home." Petra ended the call.

She stared at her phone for a minute. No, she wouldn't go home. She didn't need nor want to live with her father in order to take care of her mother. She would, however, go there this morning to visit for a while. Her father would be at work soon.

Sometimes she resented Petra with her family life and Nyx with her glamorous one. She was the middle girl with the mediocre existence who had never found her place in the world. She had followed dreams set out for her by her father's desire to have boys and children in suitable careers. Nyx had put a stop to that where she was concerned, but Ember hadn't been brave enough.

Taking this trip and quitting her job without thought had not been totally out of character for her. She had lost count of the times she leapt first then asked questions later. But, life had been leading her to this moment. Her bones ached with that truth.

She stole a glance around the small, but clean kitchen. She would take Raf up on his offer. Or maybe it was a dare. Either way, she would stay. Just to see what happened. And if she upset her father along the way, so be it. He had been upsetting people his entire life.

And if she had a little fun while she was in town, then she did. She had asked Raf what he did for fun. Staying with him would be her one fun thing. She had earned a little fun, hadn't she?

Ember unlocked the front door of her parents' house and let herself in. The shades were still drawn in most of the front rooms, casting the house in shadows. Her mother always loved the shades open even on cloudy days. She had always said seeing the sunshine, even if covered by the clouds, brought her joy. Finding the shades drawn tight made Ember's heart hurt. She would make a note to tell her father to open them before he left for work.

"Mom?" she called into the house.

No answer.

Her father's truck was not in the driveway or the garage. Like she had suspected, he had left for work early and would not be home until dinner time or later. Which meant he left her mother home alone all day. He was inconsiderate and selfish.

"Mom, are you here?" She followed the hallway to the kitchen.

This room was brighter because the kitchen faced the back of the house where the sun rose. The windows were decorated with lacy white curtains that outlined the top of each. Even the back door, the top half all glass, had nothing covering it, allowing those warm rays to swoop in and paint their hope all over the walls. Her father only allowed the lack of shades on these windows because the house backed up to a farm. Otherwise, he believed everyone was looking in at them all hours of the day and insisted the windows be covered in the evenings.

Her mom stood at the counter, wearing her red apron and squinting her eyes at an index card that would no doubt hold a baking recipe. The counter was covered with a bag of flour, the matching ceramic canister set that housed the sugar—white and brown—vanilla extract, baking powder, and the full-size mixer. The old FM radio sat on the windowsill and played a sixties station quietly in the background.

Mom's hair was wiry and sticking up in multiple directions as if her hands had been through it a few hundred times. The creases between Mom's brows had deepened over the years, and the lines around her mouth were more prominent. Her hands were dotted with the discoloration of a life lived. Her mother had aged while Ember had been busy with an existence she never really wanted—a job she never loved and a man to match. She bit back an unexpected tear at the loss of opportunities. She wasn't getting any younger. When was she going to start living the life she wanted?

"Hi, Mom." Her voice bumped against her emotions on its way out.

Her mother's head snapped up. A look of confusion crossed over her features like a scene fading to black, but recognition triumphed in the end.

"Ember. What a nice surprise. I didn't know you

were in town. When did you get in? Did you come for a long visit?"

She didn't bother telling her mother that she had been there just the day before. All that information wasn't important. "I'm in town for a while. What are you baking? Can I help?" She eased closer to the counter.

"That would be wonderful." Her mom clapped her hands. "Do you remember how we used to bake at Christmas? All those cookies." Her mom's gaze trailed off to another time and place. Probably a time when life was filled with things to do and children to chase and presents to wrap—and a mind intact.

Even with her father's heartless presence, this house was filled with love because of her mom. Mom had done her best to make them feel safe and wanted.

"Those were good times. Are you making cookies today?" She glanced around but didn't see the cookie sheets anywhere. The oven wasn't preheating either.

"I wanted to make my pecan cookies, but would you believe I couldn't remember all the steps. So silly of me, but some recipes are harder to follow than others." Mom held up the index card filled with her squiggly writing. The words had faded and worn away from so much use over the years. Some places the words were blotted out from an errant spill.

"May I?" She took the card. It was the recipe for the beloved pecan cookies. But her mother had never referred to this. The recipe only called for four ingredients and a few easy steps that her mother had taught her once without ever referencing instructions. "Without your glasses, you're probably just having trouble seeing the steps. Can I get them for you?"

"I don't need my glasses, Ember. I just wanted to refer to my recipe. It's been ages since I made these. That's all."

She hoped that was the case and not that her mother was forgetting how to read.

"Okay." She handed the card back. "How about if I pull the ingredients together and you do the mixing?"

"Sounds wonderful."

They worked side by side as the radio continued to fill the empty space. Measuring ingredients, chopping pecans, and rolling the slightly sticky dough in her hands to make balls settled a calmness over her she hadn't felt in a long time. She had forgotten how much she enjoyed baking with her mother when she was younger. Petra and Nyx hadn't taken to baking the way she had. It had become the activity she could share with her mother, keeping Mom all to herself at least for a couple hours.

As they worked, Mom seemed more like herself. They went from pecan cookies to chocolate chip because they were her favorite, and Mom had remembered.

"Mom, are all your recipes on index cards?" She put a tray in the oven. The room smelled of sugar and butter.

"Some of them. I also have a recipe book where I jotted down a few things." Mom plopped cookie dough on the tray with the ease of a professional. She had always marveled at her mother's skills in the kitchen. Petra was similar that way, but other than baking, Ember could barely make toast.

"You are an exceptional baker. Did you ever think about it as a career?" She had always wondered if her mother regretted not having a career of her own. Baking seemed like such a good fit for Mom. She poured so much love into her recipes, as if it were her secret ingredient.

"Baking? Oh, no. Never. I had three children to raise and a husband who worked around the clock. There wasn't time for me to have a career. Besides, the orchard makes baked goods. They don't need my cookies." Mom dropped the dough onto the next tray.

"They make pies and doughnuts. The pecan cookies would be nice in the fall and winter. Your lemon cookies would be a good fit in the summer. You could even make some kind of apple cookie probably. Why didn't Dad ever suggest you bake for the orchard?" And why hadn't she ever asked her mother about that before today? Because until now, she had believed her mom would go on living forever. Mom would always be in this kitchen waiting for her. Well, that was a fool's story.

"We have people working in the bakery. I never wanted to be a professional baker. I was happy being a mother."

"You could have done both." She had believed becoming a mother was not for her. She didn't trust herself to do right by a child. Picking the wrong man to build a family with was as easy as eating these cookies. Keith had been the wrong man. If she'd had children with him, they would have suffered at the hands of her bad choices.

"I didn't want to. I loved being here when you three came home from school." That wistful look passed over Mom's face again. The best years of her life seemed to be somewhere behind her, out of reach.

"You always had cookies ready. The house would smell like warm butter and sugar when we walked in."

Those hours after school when she and her sisters sat around the kitchen table doing homework and getting the treat of homemade cookies could make all the other things that were wrong with this home seem as if they belonged to someone else.

"See? If I had been baking for the orchard, you three would have come home to an empty, cold house."

"We could have come to the orchard like Brooklyn and Brad used to." In some ways, growing up, she had envied her cousins' life with their father. Silas was a very involved parent. Maybe because he was their only one. He used to bring Brooklyn and Brad everywhere. And after school, the bus would drop them off at the orchard as a favor to the family.

Once, she had jumped off the bus with them, hoping her father would be as happy to see her as Silas was to see his children, but her father had ranted and raved about her showing up. And that she belonged at home. He had made her mother come get her because he had been too busy to leave.

Her heart had shattered in a million pieces while her cousins watched her climb into the back of her mother's car. They had run off before she pulled away. They had been the lucky ones.

"Your uncle Silas didn't have a choice. That awful Patricia Sutter had abandoned her family, and those children weren't exactly safe in that cabin all alone."

"I think the cabin is cool." Her uncle had built a small cabin up the mountain and powered it with a generator. He wanted to be off the grid as much as he could be. He was eccentric. Enough that his wife had left him and their children for a different life. But Brad and Brooklyn always seemed happy as kids. They were never hurt. They knew their father loved them.

And she knew her mother loved her. So, why wasn't that enough? Why did she still hope her father would change?

"I can't imagine having to go outside to use the bathroom. He bathes in a tub where he has to bring in hot water. That was no way to raise children."

"They turned out okay. Brad practically runs the orchard and Petra told me Brooklyn bought her grandmother's alpaca farm." She would take a ride over to the farm. It would be nice to visit with Brooklyn and the alpacas. They were sweet animals full of love. She could use a little unconditional love in her life these days.

"Let's start cleaning up. I want the kitchen back in order before your father gets home." Her mother gathered the dry ingredients and shoved them in a lower cabinet.

"You're allowed to bake in your home, Mom." She wished her mother would stand up to her father for once.

"Of course I am. I'm not a prisoner here. Your father likes things orderly. And I need to start dinner."

"Why don't we do pickup tonight?"

"Not tonight. Another time. When your father has his meeting. Now, take those cookies out of the oven before they burn so they can cool. I have tins in the cabinets over the refrigerator. I'll pack some up for you to take with you."

"Mom, why do you let Dad tell you what to do all the time?" She should shut her mouth, but the same old argument forced its way out like a hurricane. She had imagined their lives without him in it a million times.

They would have been better off. Her mother would have been happier. But her mother was steadfast and true. She wouldn't leave her husband and dismantle her family.

Her mother fisted her hands on her hips. "Ember, you don't understand your father. You never have. He's way more bark than bite. I enjoy doing the things that make him happy."

"What about what makes you happy?" She tried to count to ten to keep herself from poking this fight, but counting wasn't working.

"I am happy. Enough of this conversation. I won't discuss it with you any longer. When you've been married for most of your life, then we can talk about the ins and outs of marriage. Now, take those cookies out of the oven before they burn so they can cool. I'll pack some cookies up for you."

"Mom, you just said that."

"I did not." Her mother tore off the apron and tossed it on the table. "If you'll excuse me a minute." She hurried from the room. A door slammed in the distance.

"Well, you blew that one." She plopped into the chair and ate another cookie.

Her phone vibrated. She dug it out of her pocket and found a text from Raf.

You're not here. Are you telling me no?

No to what? She couldn't resist teasing him. He wanted to know if she had decided to stay in his house. Which she had, but she wondered if he would miss her when he didn't find her there.

Have you forgotten our talk already?

She hadn't forgotten a thing. Unlike her poor mother

who had trouble remembering more and more. They had had such a nice day and she went and ruined it by pushing her mother. For a little while, their problems weren't present and she and Mom were simply spending time together like any other day.

She stared at her phone. Did she stay with Raf or did she go?

I'll stay. Need to know one thing first.

Okay.

Do you like cookies?

CHAPTER NINE

Raf wasn't up for a night out, but he had promised Ax. Maybe a few hours with the guys would take his mind off Tino who was still missing. Raf parked at the old grain farm. The main building that once housed the operations of the farm had been abandoned for decades and was recently converted into a brewery, attracting plenty of customers.

The old farmland had been cut into pieces like a sheet cake and sold off to businesses, but the property surrounding the building had remained. The brewery was on the outskirts of town on the opposite side from Main Street's activities.

Raf was glad to be off the well-used path tonight. He didn't want to accidently bump into Tino or Johnny. Assuming Tino was even in town.

The other guys were already there. Ax bounced on his toes with his hands shoved in his back pockets. Raf shook his head as he pushed out of the truck. Ax was a well-respected street artist that had morphed into more than painting buildings and train cars and still he was nervous to show his friends his picture like he used to be when he was a kid.

The stars were in the sky tonight. At least the weather had cooperated. Hopefully, it did the same when the whole town came out for the official unveiling.

Brad stood with Caleb and two of the River brothers —Malbec and Merlot. Dax Fabian, the guest of honor, was talking to someone on his phone. Once an important guy, always an important guy.

He went to high school with all these men and they were buddies of his in one form or another. Brad and Caleb hadn't spent a whole lot of time together until after Caleb started dating Brooklyn. But Merlot, Malbec, and Caleb had always been close. Strange world Candlewood Falls was.

"Hey," he said, approaching the group. He had become close with Brad after he started working at the orchard even though they had hung out once in a while as kids. He believed Brad had taken pity on him and his situation. Now, he couldn't imagine not having Brad as a friend.

"Hey, man." Brad shook his hand with his fierce grip. "Didn't think you were going to show."

"Alvarez, it's about time." Malbec gave him a shove. Because of his friendship with Brad, he got to know Malbec and Merlot. They were decent guys. Malbec worked at his family's winery, and Merlot had become a parole officer because Caleb had been accused of a murder he didn't commit.

"Looking good in that fancy shirt, Raf." Caleb poked him in the ribs. Caleb always wore a t-shirt and his motorcycle jacket, probably because Caleb had spent the better part of his adult life on the road. Not a lot of space for clothes.

"This thing? It's old." The black shirt was made with silk and it was his favorite, but he'd leave that information out because these men would never let him hear the end of it. He liked to dress nicely when he could because growing up, he had to share his clothes with Ax and Matt. Nothing was ever new or just his.

"My brother has good taste in clothes." Ax came up and gripped him in a hug. "You're late."

"Not by much." He checked his watch which was another item he had allowed himself after he started making a little money. "Okay, fifteen minutes. Sorry."

"I don't believe what I'm seeing." Dax hustled over, shoving his phone in his pocket. "Raf Alvarez, as I live and breathe. What is going on?" Dax pulled him into a half shake, half hug, slamming him on the back until he couldn't take in air.

"Are you trying to break a rib?" He shoved Dax back, who just laughed. Dax looked good. Still in shape even though he didn't play hockey anymore. The lines around his mouth had deepened, but every one of them had changed since their high school days. He was glad he wasn't the same person anymore.

"I want to say thanks to you all for coming out." Dax rubbed his thick hands together. "But especially to Ax for painting my picture. Thank you."

"Just doing my job. Are you guys ready?"

"Pull the sheet already," Merlot said.

"Okay. Okay. Here's to Dax." Axel grabbed the blue cloth that hung over the side of the building and yanked.

The cloth fluttered to the ground in a soft puddle. They took a collective breath. His chest filled with pride for his brother. Ax's talent never ceased to amaze him.

The side of the building had been transformed from a white wall with chipped paint to a masterpiece. Dax Fabian wore his professional hockey jersey. He held his hockey stick in one hand and hefted the championship trophy over his head with the other. The best part was the water Ax had painted coming out of the top of the trophy as if it were a tidal wave and then landing in a picture of a frozen lake where two silhouettes skated after a puck.

"This is great work." He didn't care what anyone thought. He grabbed Ax and hugged him to say what he couldn't in words.

"Your opinion matters the most," Ax whispered in his ear, then pulled away. "I took advantage of expression and added the water and all the background colors. The building needed a facelift anyway. But if you look, you can see several places where I included pieces of Dax's history. See there in the hockey stick?"

"Or in the top corner," Malbec said with excited enthusiasm.

"Exactly." Ax pointed at Malbec.

"And that's the shot Sports Illustrated always uses, but you didn't make it obvious." Merlot made a circle with his arm near the bottom left corner of the building.

"And I just thought you were going to slap his ugly face on the side of the building," Caleb said.

"Thank you." Dax nodded with his lips pressed in a thin line. "Thank you for making me look cool. I hope everyone in town likes it."

"They will," Raf said.

"If they don't, we're screwed. It will take a lot of paint to cover this, and I'm not giving the money back." Ax laughed.

"Let's take this party inside," Brad said. "Dax is buying the first round."

"I am?"

"You bet your ass you are. You've got all that pro hockey money burning up your wallet." Brad put an arm around Dax's shoulders and led him into the brewery.

The rest of them followed.

Raf brought three beers to the table. He had downshifted to soda since he was driving. By the looks of things, he might be driving Brad, Caleb, and Ax home. Those three fools were falling over each other, laughing at something Caleb had said. Malbec, Merlot, and Dax were in the back corner of the brewery, playing a very competitive game of pool. A lot of shouting and cursing came from over there.

The brewery was mostly open concept with a second floor that could look straight down on the first floor where they sat at a high-top table. The pool table was in the back behind the bar that took up the center space. A stage area flanked the back wall on this floor for live music.

"This is my last one." Brad held up his bottle.

"Yeah, no more for me either," Caleb said. "I can't go home drunk. Cordy is visiting us. She'll make me sleep with the alpacas if I come stumbling in the house."

Raf turned his glass in circles. He and Caleb had a lot in common when it came to upbringings. Caleb had landed on his feet too, especially when he scored Brooklyn Wilde. "Not Brooklyn?"

"Her too."

They shared a collective laugh. His mind wandered to his new roommate. She would not care at all about his state when he returned. She might not even notice if he was even there. They hadn't spoken much since the kiss. At the time, he couldn't imagine doing it. Now he couldn't think about anything else.

"I can't believe I'm about to tell you boneheads this, but I think I'm ready to propose to Lyra." Brad slugged his beer.

"It's about time," Ax said, leaning his elbows on the table as if he didn't want to miss a word of what Brad had to say.

"I know I've been dragging my feet. But in my defense, I was waiting for Winter's auntie Nora to accept the fact that she didn't get custody of Winter. All the back and forth with Nora added stress to our family that we didn't need." Brad raised a brow.

"Nora didn't have much of a choice but to concede. You never denied custody," he said. Last December had turned Brad's life around when he decided he wanted Winter to live with him. That was also around the time Lyra and her boys had moved in with Brad.

"Legally, there wasn't a lot she could do to stop me. I had copies of all the canceled checks Winter's mother had cashed over the years. And like you said, I never said I wasn't her father. Nora had a hard time losing

Winter, but she seems to be good with it now. Lyra was the one who helped her more than I did."

"That's because Lyra has a heart of gold." He punched Brad in the shoulder.

"And she's a great therapist. I'm glad she stuck with it," Brad said, rubbing his arm—more for effect. Brad's arm was all muscle. His hand probably hurt worse.

"Once she figured out why her license had not been renewed, things fell into place," Caleb said, finishing off his beer.

Everyone had assumed Lyra's ex had somehow stolen her license, but it had simply been Lyra forgetting to renew. With all that had been happening last winter, he wasn't surprised at the oversight. Anyone could've made that mistake.

A crash and a howl came from the pool table area. Malbec and Merlot rolled around, throwing punches at each other.

"Let's get those two out of here." Caleb slid off the chair.

"A little help, please," Dax shouted.

"Looks like the night's over." He left a large tip on the table. And with the help of his friends, they piled Malbec and Merlot in the car.

"Some night," Ax said, standing by his truck.

"Some night indeed."

CHAPTER TEN

The knock on the door came hard and fast. Raf put down his phone and went to see who could want him with such urgency at this time of night. Ember wasn't home. Maybe she had forgotten the key he had made for her.

"Did you—" He stopped short. Ax stood on the porch in his denim jacket with his hands in his pockets. Weariness covered his face like a mask.

"Hey, Raf." Ax's eyes were hooded.

"Hey, Ax. You okay? You want to come inside?"

"Nah, I'm good. I was wondering… have you heard from Tino?"

"I haven't heard a word from Santino. And neither has Matt. I talked to him earlier, you know, in case Tino called Matt for help." Matt had given up on Tino a long time ago. Tino had crashed Matt's car. Tino swore he wasn't drinking that night, but somehow he banged into the side of a metal bridge on a one-lane road. No other cars were there. Tino had walked away, but Matt's car was totaled, and Tino didn't even offer to help Matt out when insurance wouldn't give him enough money to replace it.

"I was wondering if you two maybe had another fight since he left."

"What gives, Axel? What aren't you telling me?" He didn't want to jump to conclusions, but the warning bells fired up in his head.

He had tried to call Tino again today, but like the last time, the call went straight to voicemail. Tino could be anywhere by now. And that was better. Still, he wanted to make sure his youngest brother was okay.

"Why don't you come outside." It wasn't a question. Ax stepped off the porch and into the shadows cast by the outdoor lights.

He followed Ax, closing the door behind him and bracing himself for what Ax would say. His mind jumped to every possible scenario—Tino robbing a convenience store this time, stealing someone's car, or worse. "You had better tell me what's going on."

Ax pointed to the side of the house where the driveway paralleled and led to the detached garage.

Had he been all wrong and this wasn't about Tino? Did Ax have a car problem? He could help his brother, but he would rather not climb under a car tonight. And when Ember came back, he would rather Ax be gone by then. He wasn't ready to explain about the pretty lady taking up residence.

He took a step in that direction, then froze. Ax did not have a car problem. "Oh, hell no." He blinked a few times to clear his vision because his eyes had to be playing tricks on him.

"Raf, listen to me for a second," Ax said.

He turned on his brother. "Shut up. Do you hear me? I told you I didn't want anything to do with him. And what did you go and do? You brought him to my home. My home, Axel. How could you?" How much pain were his brothers going to cause him? And after all the support he always gave out. For once, he wished they would think about how he might react to their bad news.

"Hello, Rafael," Johnny Alvarez said. His voice was pocked with more gravel than he remembered. His hair was streaked with gray and had thinned out. His skin sagged at his jawline. Time had not been kind to his father. Every year that Johnny had lived showed on his face.

"I've got nothing to say to you." He tried to pull his gaze away, but like a train wreck, he couldn't stop looking.

He wanted to ask all the questions that had burned in his mind. Where had he been? Why had he left? Why hadn't he been the kind of father they needed? But he said nothing. Because nothing would change if he said one single word.

The last time he saw his father he was eighteen years old. His father had left for work in the morning and never returned. He hadn't left a note or said anything except to make sure dinner was ready when he got home. That had been twenty-three years ago.

The man who in the past seemed larger than life, now had his middle pushing against the buttons of his shirt and hanging over the top of his jeans. He could look his father in the eye for the first time because he hadn't finished growing until he was twenty. After his father had left.

He had stopped being afraid of Johnny when he had learned that being a man meant sticking around and taking care of his brothers.

"Raf, I brought him by so you two could talk." Ax's words drove him from the past and crashed him back into the unwanted present moment.

"There's nothing to talk about. You walked out on us. I didn't need you then, and I sure as hell don't need you now. Get off my property, Johnny." He turned, not waiting for his father to speak.

"I'm sorry, Rafael. I'm truly sorry, son."

The words stabbed him—in the back.

∼

"Raf, your brother and some man are standing in the driveway." Ember juggled the heavy groceries into Raf's kitchen. If she was going to stay here, she needed to earn her keep. They would have to talk about rent too. She would pay her own way no matter how much she enjoyed this stroke of luck that brought her to Raf's place.

He wasn't in the kitchen or anywhere on the first floor.

"Raf, are you here?" She shrugged out of her jacket and tossed it over the chair.

Ax had said hello to her as she struggled getting out of the car with the bags, but the other guy, older and worn like leather, just stared at her with a piercing glare.

Even in the dimness of dusk and the soft glow of the porch lights, he couldn't hide his gaze.

"What's all this?" Raf sauntered into the room in his white t-shirt and jeans. His black hair fell away from his face in waves. When he smiled, his bottom lip thinned out.

She hadn't been able to stop thinking about their kiss. Those thoughts led to more questions about the feel of his broad shoulders under her touch or how lean his torso was as it tapered to those long muscular legs. She bit back a whistle. He was the sexiest man she had ever seen, and he was off-limits because he was strong and opinionated. She'd had her fill of those men. Hell, she was the daughter of one. This time around she wanted a man who did everything she said without question. *But that kiss...*

"I bought stuff to make dinner. And a few other things. Your brother is outside with some guy." She pulled the vegetables out of the bag and placed them in the fridge.

"Still? I told them to go." He went to the front of the house and cursed loud enough in Spanish it flew back toward her like a wild pitch.

"I guess you're not happy to see them."

He bounded back into the kitchen. "That other guy? The older one? He's the reason my brother Tino has so many problems. If it weren't for him, me and all my brothers would be better off." Raf paced the kitchen in a few strides.

"You seem okay to me." She liked what she saw so far. He had a good job and one he'd kept most of his life as far as she had heard. He owned his own home with space to rent out. He might have a brother with issues, but Ax had made something of himself. She had kept some tabs on the people of Candlewood Falls. Especially the ones who had succeeded so publicly. She didn't know anything about Raf's other brother. He was a bit of a mystery.

"I'm good now. I wasn't once. And Tino still isn't." He ran a hand through his hair, making the waves more pronounced. Now she wanted to touch him there too.

"Maybe that's on Tino. He's a grown-up." She unloaded the rest of the groceries and folded the bag for reuse.

"Please don't lecture me on how Tino needs to be responsible for himself, Ember. He's had a hard life. You don't know him." The smile turned to a snarl.

"Let me guess, that guy out there is your absentee father. And when he was around, he wasn't a very good one. Do I have that so far?" She could understand Raf's need to protect his brother. She felt the same way about Nyx most days because when she was little, Huck scared her so much that Nyx would often hide in her closet.

"You are correct. Johnny was about as rotten as any apple I've ever seen. And I don't want him around my house or my brothers. I don't want to debate this with you. You have no idea what it's like to have a father who failed you."

"You're right, Raf. I don't have any idea what a *less than stellar* father looks like." The sarcasm dripped off her words and landed between them.

"I'm sorry." He plopped into the chair and ran a hand over his face. "I know how difficult Huck is."

"Forget it." She wanted to. He was upset. She didn't

need to egg him on. "My phone is vibrating anyway." She wanted to ignore this call, let it go to voicemail, but she didn't want to fight with her mother anymore. If she was calling for help or to talk, she wanted to be there for her mom.

"Hello?"

"Ember Rose," her father's voice boomed through the line. She nearly dropped the phone from the shock. He never called her.

"Hello, Dad."

Raf narrowed his eyes. She gave him a shrug and turned her back.

"You have upset your mother every time you've come here this week."

"I don't mean to." Multiple times this week she had arrived at home, hoping she and her mother would be able to talk about her condition or her plans for the future, and each time Mom changed the subject or said that Dad would handle it. Every visit ended with an argument about her mother allowing Huck to control her. Mom needed to realize now, more than ever, was the time to take care of herself.

"You're doing it. Every time you're here. I can't have you coming around and getting her upset. When she gets like that, she forgets things. If you keep saying things to her that have her distraught, I will forbid you to come in this house. Am I clear?"

Like a nor'easter blowing off a roof. "How is Mom now?"

"She's upset. I told you."

"What is she doing now? Why are you on the phone with me if she's upset?" She rested her head against the window frame. The slight draft cooled her heated skin. *Go take care of her*, she wanted to scream.

"Because I want to make it crystal clear that you cannot be the reason your mother gets in one of her moods. I will not allow you to come back here and mess up what's working."

"What *is* working, Dad? Petra says nothing. I have to agree. Mom couldn't even remember a simple recipe today." Or the other day.

"You're missing the point." Her father's voice twisted with frustration.

She and her father always came to blows. "I think you are too."

"Where are you now?" he said.

"Does that matter? I'm not with you." She glanced out the window. The day had washed away, and the night had taken its place. The darkness pressed on the trees the way her relationship with her father pressed on her heart.

"Where in town are you staying? I checked with Brad and Brooklyn. You aren't with them. I also asked Lacey. She said she hasn't seen you. She didn't even know you were in town."

"I haven't had a chance to visit with her yet." She wasn't here to go down memory lane with her relatives. She was here to see how badly her mother needed help. She couldn't trust her father to do what would be required.

"Then where are you?" Each word was forced.

If she didn't tell him, he would badger her and everyone in town until he found out. He would find out. Her father had eyes everywhere. Even when she was a teenager, she couldn't do much without it getting back to him. "I'm renting space from a friend for a month or two."

"Who is this friend? Just tell me. I'll find out soon enough anyway."

She wished she was in the room with him when she made this announcement. Seeing the shocked look on his face would be worth the rupture about to happen. "I'm renting a room from Raf Alvarez."

Her father went silent.

"Dad? Are you still there?" She pulled the phone away from her ear to make sure the call was still connected and she wouldn't have to say it twice.

"No daughter of mine will take up with a man like Alvarez. He might work at the orchard, but you can't go living with him. And I don't want you anywhere near that brother of his. He's dangerous."

"I'm a grown woman. I can do as I please." And it pleased her to be with Raf even if it shouldn't. He was wrong for her. At least that's what she kept telling herself.

"You are my daughter. You will do what I say," he bellowed like a wounded animal.

"I don't need you to parent me any longer. I'm practically middle-aged. And if I want to live with Raf or screw his brains out, I can do just that." She ended the call with a scream and dropped the phone on the table.

"Screw my brains out?"

She whirled around to find Raf still sitting in the chair and smirking at her. "I forgot you were there."

"Apparently."

"I'm sorry. I shouldn't have said that. He just makes

me so mad, thinking he can tell me what to do and who I can do it with." She wasn't entirely sure telling her father about screwing Raf was a complete accident. Hadn't she been thinking about that from the moment he had walked into the kitchen tonight?

"So you put an idea about me in his head that will make it explode." He tapped his fingers hastily on the table as if he may be all out of patience.

"I wasn't thinking." Heat climbed up her neck and burned her face. She should grab her things and go see Lacey after all. At least at the bed and breakfast she wouldn't have to worry about saying the wrong thing because her mouth worked faster than her brain.

"I have to work with him, you know. He's going to hunt me down tomorrow and give me shit for offering my home to you. I'm going to have to make Brad run defense for me."

Her stomach turned. "Raf, I'll call him back and tell him I didn't mean the screwing part. That I just said it to get a rise out of him. I don't want you to have trouble at work." She had enough problems with her father. No one else needed to be dragged into their family drama.

He pushed out of the chair and cleared the space between them in two strides. He cupped her face between his calloused hands. "You will do no such thing."

And he kissed her.

CHAPTER ELEVEN

He had lost his mind.

But that didn't stop Raf from kissing Ember. His fingers were tangled in her soft hair. Her lips parted for him as her arms wrapped around his neck. He took that as a sign to keep going and dove his tongue into her mouth as if he were jumping off the high dive into pure bliss. She tasted like a cool winter morning.

Hell would rise up in the form of Huck Wilde when he found out his daughter was locked in a kiss with him. But he couldn't stop. And if Ember wanted to kiss him back, and if luck was on his side, maybe she wanted to do more. She would be the one to make the decision. After all, she did tell her father she could live her own life… and wanted to screw his brains out. Wishful thinking, but hey.

She eased out of the embrace and looked up at him with wide eyes. The blues had turned to lusty storm clouds. "You kissed me."

"Looks that way."

"I kissed you back." She ran her fingers over the back of his neck. The pressure in his jeans increased.

This woman had him wanting to take her to bed and shut out the rest of the world. He hardly knew her, might not even be good enough for her, but he was going crazy over her.

"Was kissing me a mistake?" He hoped not. But if she said yes, then he would have to back away with a ton of regret.

"Did you kiss me to make my father mad?" She worked her bottom lip under her teeth. He wanted some action on that lip.

"I can do plenty of other things at work to make your dad mad. I kissed you because I wanted to." He risked placing his hands on her hips and pulling her closer. She settled against him as if they'd practiced that move for years.

"Would you kiss me again?"

"All day long."

Ember stood on her toes to reach Raf's mouth better. If she were honest, needing to reach his mouth wasn't her motivation. She wanted a reason to press more of her body against his solid one.

His strong arms circled her and held her as if he could protect her from anything, or maybe that was her imagination because she hadn't asked for protection. As much as she had her own back, she could use someone else to lean on right now.

His lips found her neck. Ripples of lust ran over her.

Her boring life had been like the top of an undisturbed lake, but the introduction of this man shook her and now she would do anything for more of him.

"Ember, I like you." He ran a thumb over her lip, leaving his salty taste behind.

"I like you too." That was honest enough for now.

"That's good. But you're going to be living here. Should we set up some kind of ground rules for what's happening? I don't want you to regret anything. I come with a lot of baggage."

"I have never in all my forty plus years found myself wanting to have sex with someone I wasn't already involved with at least a couple of weeks. But you aren't like anyone else. I felt a strong attraction to you the minute I laid eyes on you."

"You weren't too pleased with me offering you a ride. I'm sure what you felt was more like disgust and not desire." He grabbed her hand and kissed her fingers.

"Oh, Rafael Alvarez, you know nothing about the female heart and mind. Only a man who could produce such an instant visceral reaction could make me want to undress him in his kitchen and have my way with him."

"*Dios mio*, woman. I want to carry you off to bed right now like a savage because you bring out some kind of primitive thing in me I didn't even know was there."

The front door banged opened. Raf jumped away from her and sprang into a fight stance. She swallowed her heart which had lodged in her throat.

"Rafael, we need to talk." The man with the graying hair bounded into the house and planted himself only a few feet from where they stood. The resemblance between Raf and Johnny was uncanny.

"Get out of my house." Raf stood inches from his father. Both men glared, but Raf had puffed up his chest and fisted his hands.

"I know you're upset. But please give me a chance to explain."

"I don't want to hear your excuses. You left us without a look back. I had to take care of my brothers to keep them out of foster care. I wasn't ready to become a dad at eighteen. Not that you had been doing such a bang-up job of it before then either."

"Hello." Raf's father peered around him and settled his gaze on her. "I should have introduced myself. My name is Johnny. I'm sorry to barge in and disrupt your evening. I wasn't thinking. I saw you come in here. I should have realized..."

"It's not a problem. I'll let you two talk." She could wait upstairs and if things heated back up, great. If not, maybe it wasn't meant to be. For tonight, at least.

"You're not the one leaving. He is." Raf pointed at Johnny.

She placed a hand on Raf's arm so he would look at her. "Maybe you should hear what he has to say."

"Why? How often do you want to hear what your father has to say? From the sounds of things between you two, not often."

"Listen to her, Rafael."

"I don't want to get in the middle of this family dispute. I'm going upstairs." She would not be able to convince him to see reason, and who was she to judge anyway? She hardly had a loving relationship with her father. She should leave Raf alone to make his own decisions.

"Ember, please don't go. This is our time. He doesn't get to barge into my house and demand I speak with him. I'm not a kid anymore."

"He has a point," she said to Johnny.

"Yes, of course. I wasn't thinking. I'm sorry. I was upset and thought I could convince you to give me five minutes. But I don't deserve to demand anything. Axel tried to warn me, but I let my emotions get the best of me. I apologize—to both of you. Excuse me." Johnny turned on his heel and went out the way he came, closing the door quietly behind him.

Raf turned to her. "How did you do that?"

"Do what?"

"Get him to listen to you. He wouldn't back down until you said I had a point. He has never walked away from an argument so easily."

"He left because you wanted him to. It was what you wanted, wasn't it?"

Raf stared at the door.

"Raf?"

He turned back to her again with a blank look on his face. She worried for a second he might be in shock.

"You wanted him to go, right?"

"Right. Sure. Of course I did. I don't want him here or to have anything to do with him."

He might believe what he said, but she wasn't so sure he was telling the truth.

CHAPTER TWELVE

R af poured coffee into a travel mug and secured the lid. The sun hadn't quite made its way into the world for the day, but the temperature promised to be mild. He'd be able to get a lot of work done if he could keep his mind on the tasks and not on how Ember responded to his kiss. Or how he'd responded to her presence when she'd walked into his kitchen this morning, still groggy from sleep. All he had wanted to do was pull her in his arms and kiss her fully awake.

Her light-brown hair tumbled around her face. Her blue eyes were hooded. Her legs were bare beneath a t-shirt that hung just below her hips. He would gladly give her one of his shirts to sleep in.

"I made enough for you too." He held up the pot. Normally, he didn't bother with coffee, but he wanted to linger a little longer at home in case she woke up before he left. Luck had been on his side this morning.

"Thanks." She grabbed a mug from the cabinet as if she'd put the set there herself. The idea pleased him, but he brushed the thought away. This thing between them moved like a meteor and was bound to burn up before they got too far. How could something moving this fast, stick?

"Are you going to talk to your dad today?" she said.

"Let's save that conversation for after coffee, okay?" He had no intentions of speaking to Johnny today or any other. If he came to town to visit Ax, there was nothing he could do about that. If Ax wanted to try again with Johnny, that was on Ax. And Ax would have to deal with the consequences when Johnny ruined everything. Because he would.

"You should give him a chance." She eyed him over the mug.

"So should you. With your dad, I mean." He couldn't believe he was even saying that because Huck was as difficult as they came. All of his children had run away from Candlewood Falls and he had practically run Brooklyn's fiancé out of town, but thankfully Caleb was more stubborn than Huck, because Huck had been very wrong about Caleb.

"You know my father. You know what he's like. And your father apologized. I've never heard my father say *I'm* and *sorry* in the same sentence."

"You don't understand. My father disappeared and now all of a sudden he shows up at Ax's place. If I had to guess, it's because Ax made something of himself and Johnny wants a piece of it." His father had always been looking for the next get rich quick scheme. He would have been a lot more financially sound if he had tried keeping a job and supporting his kids.

"You aren't one for second chances, are you?" She lowered into the chair and tucked her legs under her.

"Depends." He forced his gaze away from her toned legs and back to her face so he could stay focused on what he had planned to say next. "I have something to ask you."

"You're changing the subject."

She could see right through him. He wasn't sure if he disliked her ability or if it turned him on. "I'm done talking about Johnny Alvarez for the day. I have more important things to think about."

"Yeah, like what?" A playful smile tugged at her lips.

"Would you like to go out with me?" The words rushed out of him like an overflowing river.

After Johnny had left, ruining the mood between him and Ember, she had taken a call from her sister. He had made a quick dinner, which she hadn't joined him for, and when he called it a night and went to bed, she hadn't come out of her room. He had contemplated knocking on her door, but then decided asking her out on an official date would be best. He wouldn't take advantage of the fact she had moved into his house.

"On a date? You're asking me out on a date?" She smoothed her hair down.

"Yes, Ember. On a date. Would you?"

"This is because we kissed."

"It has something to do with it." He tried to hide his disappointment. She was stalling, probably because she didn't know how to tell him she didn't want to. "Is that a no, then?"

She unfolded from the chair and crossed the room to

him. Her fingers traced his jaw and settled on his shoulders. He forced his hands to stay put. He wasn't sure what was happening and he didn't want to blow it.

"You don't have to take me out to kiss me again." Her voice dropped a sultry octave.

He swallowed the desire building inside him. He would not start something now. He had to get to work and he wanted their first time—and he was pretty sure there'd be a first time—to be more special than a quick romp in the kitchen. They could do that later when they had been together a while.

He let out a long breath. He needed to slow the hell down, but she made him want to run head first into the abyss. She wasn't like any other woman he had known.

"I think the right thing to do would be to take you out in public. Let's make sure we have more than just chemistry."

"What's wrong with chemistry?" Her fingers traced his arm. He wanted her hands other places too. She was making him forget about needing to get to work.

"Absolutely nothing. In fact, it's a requirement. But I'm not the kind of man who rents out a room and then takes advantage of his roommate. Either go out on a date with me, or we won't be kissing again." He hated to make that ultimatum, but he wanted to treat her the way she deserved.

She stepped back. "You drive a hard bargain."

"I'll take that as a yes, then. I'll pick you up tonight at six."

"Are you going to pick me up here in the kitchen?"

"I'll come to the door. Be ready." He would stop at

Brad's for a shower. He had already packed a change of clothes and thrown them in the truck this morning, hoping she'd say yes to him.

"Where are we going?"

"I'll surprise you." He had no idea where he would take her, but he'd figure it out.

"What if I don't like surprises?"

"Now is a good time to start."

Ember needed a car. Taking the driving service was getting costly and she needed to watch her money over the next month. That was how long she would give herself to come up with a plan for her mom and to figure out what she wanted to do for work. Because her IT days were over.

She cleaned up the coffee mugs and went upstairs to take a quick shower. The extra bathroom in the hallway was simple with white and black tiles on the floor, white subway tiles around the tub, and one white sink with a gray marble counter. Easy on the eyes—like Raf. The towels under the sink were white and thick. She brought one to her nose and inhaled deeply, smelling his spicy scent and a hint of laundry detergent. She turned on the water and tried not to picture Raf standing there with her.

She hadn't planned to reinvent herself at forty-one, but she rarely planned anything. Her impatience often brought her problems, but maybe this time was different because the one thing she seemed to have was a very handsome man interested in her. Her breakup with Keith was still new, but in truth they had grown apart a long time ago. Keith was in love with work. Not with her. She wanted someone who would put her needs first once in a while.

"Oh, Ember, you need to deal with your daddy issues," she said to the empty room. She groaned at how pathetic she was.

Last night Nyx had called her to see how Mom was getting along. Her younger sister was doing her best to stay involved, but her life as a country singer made it difficult to be close. Nyx often helped in other ways. She always opened her wallet. And she was doing it again. She was having a car delivered to Raf's this morning. Nyx had rented it for the month for her so she could get around town.

She turned off the water and dried off, wanting to linger a little longer under the soft cotton, but the car would arrive soon and she was headed back to her parents' house today. She hoped that maybe she and her mom could bake something else.

Baking made sense when so many other things didn't. Following a recipe meant that at the end, something good and delicious would be the reward. Baking provided a kind of guarantee that life often couldn't.

She had never expected her mom to get sick so young, or at all. She had foolishly thought they would have all the time in the world, but they didn't. And she needed to let some of her resentment go. She had wanted her mother to leave her father and start over, just the four of them. They would have been fine, but her mother stayed and let her and her sisters go away.

A car honked outside. She ran for the door to find a

blue Prius in the driveway and a man in black pants and a black button-down waving to her as she stepped onto the porch.

"Hi, I'm Ray. I work at the rental place. I'm dropping off a car for Ember Wilde." He consulted a piece of paper, then looked back at her with a crooked smile.

"That's me." She nearly skipped to the car, but she forced herself to act like an adult. Her sister had come through.

"Great. Here are the keys. The tank is full. Your return date is on the form." He handed her the yellow piece of paper.

"How are you getting back?" There were no other cars around.

"My ride will be here soon. Hey, can I ask you something?" He checked the form again.

"Sure."

"The person who paid for the rental was Nyx Wilde. Like the country singer. You're not related, are you?"

"That's my sister." She was often asked if there was a relation. She never minded and wondered how Raf felt about having a brother with certain amount of fame. Something else they had in common.

"Wow. I love her music. Are you related to the people who own the orchard too?" His eyes grew to the size of sunflowers.

"Yup. That's us. One big happy family." On the surface, anyway.

"You guys are the luckiest. It's just me and my sister. We don't do anything as cool as your family."

"It's all perspective, Ray."

"Yeah, and from my viewpoint, your family is all

looking up." He gave a short wave and waited at the road until another car arrived and he jumped in.

"Family isn't all it's cracked up to be," she said to herself. She wanted to say that to Ray, but he was a stranger and wouldn't understand that sometimes you aren't born to the right people. And success at work didn't guarantee success in all parts of your life.

She should know.

Ember let herself into the house. "Mom?"

The rooms were dark again. She went around and opened all the shades, allowing the warmth and the promising sunlight into the house. The golden rays filled with a million tiny dust particles that she had disturbed.

"Mom?"

The kitchen was quiet. The dish board was filled with clean dinner plates and two glasses and a pot. The sink was as empty as the room.

She followed the stairs to the second floor and the four bedrooms. She had been grateful she never had to share a room while growing up. At least she had a small space she could escape to when she needed to hide. In her teen years that had seemed like all the time.

"Mom, are you here?" She nudged her parents' bedroom door open, but the room was also empty. The bed was made, and a blue silk robe was draped over the arm of tufted chair in the corner.

She hadn't planned on her mother being out. Her heart picked up pace, and her breath shallowed. She was overreacting and dug her phone out of her pocket to call her father.

"Huck Wilde."

She restrained a sigh. He must see her number on the screen. He had to know who it was. Or was he just that oblivious? "Hi, Dad. I'm at the house. Mom isn't here. Did she have plans today?" It might have been nice to know before she came out here, but where else was she going to go? To the orchard to hang out with Raf? She didn't think so.

"What do you mean she isn't home?"

"I've been through the house. She isn't here."

"Go look for her. She might be down the street near the park. I'll be right there." He hung up.

The park? She hurried out of the house and ran toward the park that she had played at as a child. All the equipment was blue and yellow. And when she got older, she would go there with her friends at night when no one was around, and they'd pop open bottles of beer.

The park came into view. She couldn't remember the last time she was here, but the years had worn down the playground like old treads on a sneaker. The equipment had lost its luster and was pocked with rust. The grass and weeds had forced their way through the dirt like pockets of unruly hair. The swing set longed for a companion.

Her mother sat by herself on the bench, staring into space. Her skin was slack, and she looked older than her years. Ember's heart tumbled in her chest.

She approached her mother as if she were a small bird that had fallen out of a tree. "Mom, what are you doing here?"

Her mother blinked and looked up. "I was waiting for my girls. They come here right after school. I bring them a snack, and I watch them as they run around. But I must have the wrong day. No one is here. What day is it?"

She sat beside her mother and took her cold hand. "Mom, it's Ember. I'm here."

"My special Ember." Her mom squeezed her hand and relaxed against the back of the bench. A wistful smile crossed her lips.

When she was young and she had a bad day at school, she would come home and tell her mother all about it. Usually, Mom had a cookie and a glass of milk for her while she spilled about the injustices of middle school.

She had never really fit in with the other kids. She was the creative one who liked to make things out of duct tape and yarn. She painted dreams on used cardboard boxes and made clouds out of cotton that she taped to her ceiling. Her mother always told her it was okay to be different, but she didn't listen. She had allowed the fear of angering her father to dictate her grown-up choices. For the first time, she wondered if Mom was trying to tell her to be different than she was.

"Are Petra and Nicole coming?" Mom said, dragging her away from the memories.

"Not today." The question stung even though it shouldn't. Mom was simply asking for her other children, but they weren't here and wouldn't be. Nyx hadn't been home in twenty-five years. Petra came at holidays and birthdays, mostly.

She had been the one who popped in from time to

time to help out with things like setting up the cable box or the new computer. She came to show her mother how to use her new smartphone or take her to lunch.

Her mother didn't like to ask for help, which was why Mom never relied on her nieces and nephews. Ember wondered if her cousins ever even thought of her mother who was lost in the hurricane of her father and this illness.

The clouds rolled in uninvited and covered the sun. The wind picked up and blew under her sweater. Her mother shivered.

"Let's go home," Ember said.

"Oh no, let's stay until the girls come."

"Mom, they aren't coming." She fought to keep the frustration out of her voice. Her mother couldn't help what she said. And still, she was angry because she couldn't help her mother the way she wanted to.

A beat-up pickup truck skidded to a stop at the curb. The diesel engine spewed its stink into the damp air. Her father jumped out and shuffled to them with his arms pumping.

The passenger door opened too. Uncle Silas pushed out of the truck. He sauntered over as if this were any family get-together. He had his hands in the pockets of his barn jacket. His jeans were smudged with dirt. The years had creased his face, but he was still as handsome as she remembered. He smiled as he approached. But he didn't come all the way to them.

"Ruby, what are you doing here?" Dad huffed and puffed as he stood before them. His face was splotched with red as he gulped for air.

"Oh, Huck. I thought today was the park day." Mom blinked back the tears forming in her eyes.

"I told you to stay home until I came back." He gripped his wife under the arm and helped her to stand.

"I looked at the clock. It was time for the park." Mom turned to her. "Huck makes the best grilled cheese."

She didn't respond, but her mom was right about that even if the comment was out of place. Her mom would do that sometimes. She would say random things as if the person she was speaking to would have no idea.

"It's not even noon," he said. "You're too early for the park, darlin'. I told you I'd take you after work. You have to promise me you'll stay home. I can't help you if you go walking around town now." His voice hitched and he wiped his eyes with the back of his hand.

Never in her life had she heard her father use a term of endearment or show any tender emotion toward his wife. For a moment, she didn't recognize him, as if he'd transformed into a completely different person and she was eavesdropping on strangers.

She shook her head to bring her parents back into focus. "She's okay, Dad. She was just sitting here."

Her father's gaze fell on her as if he just noticed she was there. "She can't go out. She knows this."

"Maybe she forgot." She pushed off the bench and stood beside her mother.

"Who forgot?" her mom said.

"Never mind that," Dad said. "I'll get you back to the house where you're safe."

"I can take her if you need to get back to work." She wanted to help in some small way.

Her father waved her words away. "Those people

answer to me and my brothers. If I say I need to be gone for a while, then I'll get back when I'm good and ready. Silas, ride with Ember back to the house. Then I'll take you back to the orchard."

"Hello, Ember," Uncle Silas said.

"Hi, Uncle Silas. It's nice to see you." She might actually mean that. Silas was the youngest of her father's brothers and the one brother her father would listen to. Silas had done his best to keep Huck from doing too many things he would regret.

Her father put an arm around her mother and pulled her close. Mom laid her head on Dad's shoulder and leaned into him as they made their way across the playground. At the truck, Dad kissed Mom on the forehead and helped her in. Even from the distance, she could tell her father was being gentle with her mother.

"He loves her," Uncle Silas said.

"He's had a funny way of showing it." He'd had a lifetime to express his love. It had to take her mother getting sick to break him. She may have witnessed a different side of her father, but she wasn't ready to forgive everything.

"Emotions were never Huck's strong point." Silas shrugged.

"That's no excuse."

"No, but a man like him was told to buck up. Our parents are good people, and now that our father is old, he's sweeter than he was as a young man raising five boys and running an orchard. Farming is hard work. There isn't time for a lot of emotions when there are trees to grow, apples to take care of, and mouths to feed. Skip didn't have a lot of patience when one of us fell down crying. That kind of stuff was our mother's arena."

"Doesn't make it right."

"But it makes it true. Can you drop me back at the orchard? I think Huck will be a while at home."

She had planned on spending time with her mother, but she would rather be there when her father wasn't. And now she had an excuse to stop by the orchard. "Sure, Uncle Silas. I'd be glad to."

CHAPTER THIRTEEN

R af tossed some of the pruning tools into the wheelbarrow. The crew had their orders to spray the trees that had begun dropping their flowers, preventing disease from taking hold. New trees were being planted this spring as well. Brad was marching up and down the rows, barking at everyone who wasn't doing something right, which was usually Raf's job, but Brad liked to be a hands-on boss.

Now was a good time to take a break. He wanted to search for a place to take Ember to dinner. He'd borrow the computer in Brad's office and maybe grab some lunch before Brad started yelling for him.

He parked the wheelbarrow inside the tool shed and wiped his hands on his jeans. He would definitely need to get cleaned up before his date tonight. He didn't want to scare Ember off by having her see him filthy before he had a chance to win her over. As crazy as it seemed, he liked her, liked thinking about her, and was lucky that she'd taken him up on his offer to rent the room from him.

As much as he wanted a tenant for the other house, the damage to the place still needed to be fixed. He hadn't had the time yet to do it himself. He had better make the time or he'd be footing the full mortgage with no end in sight. Just the property taxes were enough to choke the life out of his bank account.

His phone vibrated against his leg. He dug it out and found a text from Ax. *Need to ask a favor.*

He bit back a curse. *What's up?*

Is your apartment still available?

Tino can't move back in.

Not Tino. Dad.

Hell no. He turned his phone off and shoved it back in his pocket. All those spray paint fumes had ruined Ax's brain. He was out of his mind if he thought Johnny could live in his house. He owed his father nothing.

He continued around the side of the market where they sold apples, honey, and merchandise. The parking lot was empty except for a blue Prius. The passenger door opened and Silas Wilde unfolded from the small car like origami.

Raf stood stock-still. He didn't recognize the car, but whoever it was somehow knew Silas well enough to give him a ride. Which was strange because Silas basically kept to himself.

"Hey, Silas," he said.

"Raf," Silas said with a nod. "Brad out in the field?" Silas would not offer any extra information or even wait around to introduce him to the person in the car. If the person even got out. He'd have to ask Brad if his father had started dating. The driver appeared to be a woman.

"He's out there scrutinizing the spraying. Basically, making everyone's life a little harder."

Silas laughed and shook his head. "I'll see what's going on."

"Who—"

"Hi, Raf." Ember cut him off before he could finish asking who was in the car with him.

Her pretty painted-red smile brightened her face. Her hair fell over the shoulder of her black sleeveless blouse that stopped at the top of her dark jeans, hugging her hips. He was a little jealous of the gold necklace lying flat against her skin.

"Where did you get that car?" He couldn't stand the space between them and cleared it so she was only inches away.

He was drawn to her like steel to a magnet. The warning bells crashed in his head until it hurt. Her father would never accept him. A family had influence on a relationship, and Huck would do whatever he could to get in between them. He should keep things platonic and save himself inevitable heartache. He had enough to worry about with Tino missing and his father's return. Yet here he was, his insides radiating as she smiled up at him.

"My sister Nyx rented the car for me. She felt guilty for not being able to come home to help out with my mom. To make herself feel better, she spends her money."

"That's not so terrible. Ax has helped out Tino by sending him money. Ax saves me from having to do it all the time." Matt would rather cut his own throat than help Tino, so he had stopped asking his brother to chip in. "Did Silas call you for a ride? I didn't know you kept in touch with him. Brad never mentioned it."

"I haven't. He came with… never mind. It's not important. It's chilly out." She rubbed her arms, changing the subject.

He would take the hint. Her life was her business. "That's April for you. I just hope we've seen the last of the frost. The apple trees don't like being cold either. Hey, I'm glad I caught you. I was about to grab lunch. Do you want to join me?"

She hitched a thumb over her shoulder. "I want to get back to Mom. My father leaves her alone all day, and she shouldn't be." She hesitated. "Can I ask you something?"

"Shoot."

"How do you know when to step in and take over and when to let things play out?"

"I think I need more information." He kind of felt that way where Tino was concerned. He wanted to grab Tino by the shoulders and shake him loose. And he also knew he had to let Tino figure things out for himself. If he ever did.

As for his father, there was nothing left to play out. Johnny had dealt his last card when he took off.

"Forget what I said. I'm just babbling." She shook her head as if she was shaking her thoughts away. "I'll see you later. I'm looking forward to tonight."

"Me too." He eased closer, hoping she wouldn't send him away. He understood she needed to be with her mom, but he would have liked to spend a little time with her this afternoon.

She placed a hand on his chest, either not noticing

how dirty he was or not caring. Her touch burned right through his work shirt. She pressed her lips to his and shifted the ground under him.

Like a starving man who found food, he couldn't wait and pushed her lips apart. She opened to him willingly and slid her tongue against his. Her arms came up around his neck and pulled him closer. Her heat mixed with his in all the places their bodies touched, like the sun and the earth. He should stop them, out here where anyone could walk up on them and see exactly how he felt about this woman. Brad would never let him hear the end of it. And he had too much respect for Ember to have her uncle or her cousins finding her in a compromising position with him, but that magnetic force was too strong.

The rumble of the engine should have been his first clue. The screeching of brakes was a solid second. But that still didn't stop him.

"Ember Rose, what the hell is going on here?" Huck yelled loud enough the birds flew from the trees and shook the earth.

They jumped apart as if they'd been burned. And basically, they had.

"Dad," Ember said, wiping her mouth with the tips of her fingers. He tried not to laugh.

Huck shoved himself between Ember and him and poked a finger in his chest. "Alvarez, I should tear you to pieces. Who do you think you are, taking advantage of my daughter like that?"

Raf threw his hands in the air and backed up. If it had been any other man, he would have stood his ground, even pushed back, but this was Huck. Not only did Huck have the power to fire him, to make his life miserable in town, but he was Ember's father and she deserved him trying to be respectful to her father.

"Dad, stop it." Ember pulled on Huck's arm, but he didn't budge.

"Calm down. Nothing was happening that everyone didn't want." He could admit the location wasn't the best place, but he wouldn't apologize for kissing a woman who wanted him to.

Huck turned on Ember. "You wanted him to kiss you?"

"Dad, stop yelling. The whole orchard will hear you."

"I don't care who hears me. No daughter of mine will get involved with a man named Alvarez. Do you hear me?"

"Hey, now. That's enough." He wouldn't stand there and be disparaged because of his heritage.

"You are nothing. And just because my brother and nephew think you're something, doesn't mean it's true. I know all about your history and that useless father of yours who's come back to town. You're just lucky you didn't end up in prison like he did." Huck poked him in the chest again.

"Huck, shut up while you still can." His heart hammered against his ribs. He forced himself to keep his hands at his sides and not break Huck's finger in two.

Johnny had been in prison. He didn't know that until now, and he wouldn't give Huck the satisfaction of being the one to tell him. That explained some of Johnny's absence, but it didn't excuse it.

"Hey, what's going on here?" Brad stomped over and stood by his side.

Huck retreated. Brad was much bigger than Huck and the only other person Huck thought twice about going up against.

"I've got it," he said without looking at Brad.

"I know you do." Brad squared his shoulders.

"It's none of your business, nephew."

"It is when it's on my orchard."

"My orchard." Huck pointed to himself. "You might be in charge of operations, but I am an owner."

Brad sneered. "Ask me if I care about that. My father is an owner too. And Uncle Cooper, and Sam and Lacey own Uncle SJ's share. And when you least expect it, I'll own a piece of this place too. Whatever your beef is with one of my men, your beef is with me. So, unless Raf stole money out of your wallet, I suggest you take a walk."

Ember covered her face with her hands. He wanted to reach over and lace her fingers through his. He hadn't meant to embarrass her. He should have controlled himself better.

Hawk scowled at Brad, then turned to Raf. "Stay away from my daughter."

"Dad, you can't tell me who to hang out with."

"He's beneath you, Ember Rose." Huck didn't wait for Ember to say anything else. He stormed away without looking back.

Brad patted him on the shoulder. "Are you okay? What got him so riled up?"

"It's nothing I can't handle. Don't worry about it." If he looked at Ember, he would give them away. She had been through enough thanks to him.

"We were kissing," Ember said.

Brad raised an eyebrow. He was pretty sure his

jumped up too. Nothing seemed to rattle her. She laid it all out on the table. He wasn't like that. He held his cards close, watching for the danger.

"My father caught us shoving our tongues down each other's throats. I'm sorry, Raf. He'll get over it."

"Man, I don't wish to be you right now," Brad said. "But hey, if you two want to kiss, make out, whatever, good for you. If you need any help with Huck, let me know."

"I'm good, thanks."

"Okay. I'm heading out. Winter has a school thing, and I promised to be sitting in the front row. I can't be late or Winter gets to paint my fingernails pink." Brad rolled his eyes. "Lyra has already texted me twice. See you guys later." Brad hurried away to the employee parking lot.

"Who is Winter?"

"That's a story for over dinner. If you still want to go, that is." He wouldn't blame her if she changed her mind.

"You bet your ass I do. I'm not letting him stop me. In fact, I want to go more."

"Hey, I don't want to be thrown in the middle." He didn't want to be someone she used to piss off her father.

"Of course not. I meant what I said this morning. I like you, Rafael. I don't care what my father thinks. He's a narrow-minded jerk who hates everyone, including me."

"He doesn't hate you. All that exploding was because he loves you and thinks I'm not good enough for you. I know it's because I'm Spanish and Huck doesn't like anyone with any kind of obvious ethnicity. He doesn't like people who don't have an education or have spent any time in prison."

"Have you spent time in jail?"

"Me? No. But my brother Tino did, and Tino stole from the orchard. I begged Brad not to send him away. Huck is mad as hell about that. But Brad honored what I asked. He's like a brother to me. He and Silas were the family I needed when I was eighteen and left alone to care for my brothers."

"My father doesn't get to decide who is in my life. I want to give us a chance. If you do too, then pick me up tonight at six. If you can't handle my father, then I'll have my bags packed, and I'll be gone by the time you get home. Just say the word."

If he were smart, he'd tell her to pack her bags. He needed to straighten out his own problems. Adding a relationship that most likely wouldn't work was another headache he could do without. She had come into his life like a storm. She would leave as quickly and have caused a whole lot of damage to his heart. He didn't see this thing between them ending any other way.

She stared at him with wide eyes, waiting for an answer.

"The word is six. I'll pick you up at six."

CHAPTER FOURTEEN

E mber closed the door to her mother's bedroom with a soft click. The afternoon had worn Mom out, and she wanted to sleep. The truth was the afternoon had worn Ember out too. Finding her mother sitting alone at the park had broken her heart into a million pieces. The vibrant, smart lady was withering away. She would be a shell of herself someday, and no one knew when that would happen. The unknown was the most frightening part.

She would have to talk to her dad about bringing someone in a few hours a day to keep an eye on Mom. She could do it while she was in town, but she had no long-term plans to stay, and even if she decided to stay, she would have to go back to work.

She padded into the kitchen and grabbed Mom's recipe book. The cover was cloth and worn from years of hands leaving oily marks. She found her mother's apron behind the door and pulled it over her head. She ran her hands over the fabric as if it would bring Mom closer.

Memories of Mom, that is. She fought back the tears while she pulled out the bowls and cookie trays.

With all the ingredients for her mom's special sugar cookies, she lost herself in the steps and directions. She dug her hand into the coolness of the flour, letting it spill over her fingers and coat them. She softened the butter and measured out vanilla, stopping to inhale its strong scent. She dropped teaspoonfuls on the well-used cookie sheets.

By the time she slid the warm cookies into containers, the tension in her body had drifted away, replaced by the satisfied ache of used muscles. She could live with the consequences of hard work, but the stress from her family drained every ounce of her energy like a greedy monster wanting to suck and lick every last morsel.

She cleaned the kitchen and checked on Mom, who was still asleep. Ember wanted to be gone before her father returned. She left a note for Mom that said goodbye and she would see her tomorrow.

The kitchen door swung open. She held her breath as her father filled the doorway, much the way she used to when she was a child whenever he returned home. Instead of being the kind of daughter who could run into her father's arms, expecting to be lifted up and spun around, she had held her breath and prayed he wouldn't come looking for her. Especially if he was in a bad mood, which had been often.

"You're still here," he said, stating the obvious.

"I was about to leave. Mom's asleep."

"You baked."

"I cleaned up everything. You don't have to worry.

And I left some cookies in the red tin on the counter." She tried to push past him.

He gripped her shoulder. "Thank you for going to the park today."

The comment stunned her like an elbow to the eye. "Don't thank me, Dad. I did it for her."

"I know you did, but thank you just the same."

"Thanking me doesn't change what you said to Raf today. That was inexcusable. He's a good man. You have to know that. You've known him for years."

She was nineteen when Raf had appeared at the orchard. Back then she had no interest in what went on there and had long since forgotten the young man who'd prowled the halls of the high school.

Her father had complained about the new hire daily, but she had never paid much attention. What would her life look like now if for only one moment she had walked onto the orchard and found Rafael amongst the apple trees? Would he have taken hold of her heart? Or would she have been too afraid to cross her father?

"He's a hard worker and he's smart. I'll give him that. He's never caused a lick of trouble at the orchard, and believe me, I watched for it. But that brother of his is trouble and he's going to end up in jail or dead, that one. And his other brother sprays graffiti all over the place. What kind of man destroys public property like that? You don't want any part of that family."

"Ax is a street artist. He makes a very good living at what he does. You don't understand art. You dislike Raf because he's Spanish."

"He's not like us."

"I don't know. I think he's a lot like us. He loves the

orchard just like you do. He works hard. He loves his family and would do anything for them. He owns a home. He's never been to prison. Doesn't seem to have a drug addiction. What's missing, Dad? Can you tell me?"

"I'm too tired for this conversation, Ember Rose. I have to get dinner ready for your mother. Do what you want. You always do anyway. Just don't say I didn't warn you." He hobbled through the kitchen as if he had aged twenty years in an afternoon.

She didn't want to admit she had noticed the dark circles under his eyes or the sagging skin around his mouth. His gaze searched the kitchen as if he hadn't a clue what he was supposed to do next.

"Do you want help making dinner?"

"I don't need help." He pressed his hand into his lower back and stooped to grab a pot.

"Okay, then." She wouldn't stay where she wasn't wanted. The stubborn old man could make his own dinner and throw his back out in the process for all she cared.

"You'll be back tomorrow, then?" he said without looking at her.

"Yes. Will you have time tomorrow to talk about Mom's care?" They needed to have this conversation now. It would take time to find the right person.

"I care for your mother."

"When you're not here." And when he couldn't any longer.

"Today was a fluke."

"It's going to happen again." And again and again.

"I don't need your help. If that's why you came home,

then go back to the city. And if I do need help, I have my family."

"What about me, Dad? Aren't I your family?"

"You know you are."

"Then why doesn't what I want for Mom count?"

"Because she's my wife. And I will be the one who takes care of my wife while there is still air in my lungs. I owe her that much, damn it." He covered his face with his hands. "Go, please. Just go."

Her hand reached out to him, but she yanked it back. She let herself out instead, the tin of cookies still tucked under her arm.

Raf turned into his driveway and laughed. He couldn't believe he was pulling up to his own house to take Ember out to dinner. But he wanted this night to feel like a real date and just having her come down the stairs didn't seem right. They had plenty of time for nights like that in the future. He shook his head. Not four months ago he had busted Brad for falling fast for his neighbor, a very unlikely companion too, and here he was doing the same thing.

The headlights caught Ax's car parked alongside the house. Dusk filtered out the day's colors except for a hint of red dropping behind the rolling hills. He turned off the truck and the light went with it.

His brother leaned against the back bumper with his arms crossed. He didn't have time for a conversation with Ax about letting Johnny live in his apartment. He had enough of fathers today after his encounter with

Huck. At least Huck had avoided him the rest of the day by staying in the offices and not coming out to the fields.

He hopped out, needing to make this quick. He wanted to go to the door like a gentleman and ring the bell. If Ember saw him out here talking with Ax, she would just come right out. Her independent side wouldn't allow her to wait for him to knock.

He stopped short. The man leaning against the car wasn't Ax.

"What are you doing here?" He checked over his shoulder to make sure Ember hadn't come out.

"I wanted to see you and ask if I can rent the one side of your house." Johnny pushed off the car. His beige fleece button-down fit to his form. A pack of cigarettes outlined the inside of the shirt pocket.

"I told Ax I don't want you here. What is it going to take to get through to you? You and I are done, old man." He had waited every day for his father to come back. He had been a boy then, completely unprepared to take care of his brothers.

He hadn't had a decent job and was a month away from high school graduation. He had planned to go to community college so he could work somewhere that didn't require him to get dirty all day. He wanted a chance to get away from the desperate side of Candlewood Falls. The side that people like Caleb Ransom understood firsthand.

Life had been hard, losing his mother when he was ten to a drug overdose. She hadn't loved them enough to clean up. Oh, he knew now as a grown man that the drugs had a hold on her. But that little boy had believed for a very long time that his mother didn't love him.

Johnny held his hands up in surrender. "Rafael, please just give me a minute. Hear me out. If you still say no, then I'll go. I promise."

He checked the time on his phone. He still had five minutes. Hopefully, Ember wouldn't look out the window and see his truck. "Okay, fine. One minute."

"I'm sorry I left you without an explanation. That was wrong. I knew that almost immediately, but there was nothing I could do. I thought about coming back, but before I could change my mind I had been arrested for a bunch of stupid things I never should have done."

"You've been in jail all this time?" He still shook from the shock of learning his father had been to prison, though he shouldn't be surprised. It seemed as if Tino had followed in Johnny's footsteps quite well.

"Not the whole time. Fifteen years. When I got out, I knew you deserved a better father than me. I didn't want you having me hanging around your neck. I had nothing to offer you and your brothers. You were all making it okay. I had checked. You were working at the orchard. Axel had made something of himself. Matias was living his life. Santino seemed the most like me, but he had you. And you were a better father than I ever was. So, I went west."

"Being their father wasn't my plan. You left me no choice."

"I knew you would step up and do the right thing. You are a good man, Rafael. You gave your brothers what I couldn't."

"What does any of this have to do with you living here?" He didn't need to rehash the past. The old stories were better left forgotten.

131

"I'm clean and sober eight years. I have a trade and a little money now. I can pay your rent, and I can fix up the damage Santino caused. I'll pay for all of that too. The materials, everything."

"Why would you do that?"

"Because you're my son, and I love you. I know I wasn't good to you when you needed it most, but please let me have a chance to make some things right."

"Why are you in Candlewood Falls?" The minute was up, but he couldn't walk away. He needed to understand what Johnny's motives were so he could be prepared for whatever crap he threw.

"Because you, Axel, and Santino are here."

"We don't know where Tino is." And if Tino was in Candlewood Falls, having Johnny around would be no good for him. Tino needed to deal with his demons, and Johnny was the biggest one.

"He'll come back. And I'm hoping Matias will talk with me."

"Good luck with that one." Matt was the most stubborn of them all. He had closed the door to the past a long time ago and had no intention of opening it again.

"He will if you ask him to."

"And if you're living in my house and fixing up the mess Tino caused, you think I'll help you out." He would not be the mouthpiece to convince Matt to speak with Johnny. Every one of his brothers could decide for themselves what to do with this man who wanted a second chance he didn't deserve.

"Perhaps."

"I don't owe you anything, Johnny."

"No, you don't. But I'm hoping you'll give me a

chance. You have a big heart, Rafael. I'm counting on that."

"Oh, for fuck's sake. I'm not taking care of your messes anymore. I already did that. I came in and cleaned up what you couldn't. I became the father my brothers needed when you were too much of a loser to do it yourself. Don't ever ask me to fix your problems with my brothers again."

"Raf?" Ember stood on the driveway behind him, staring at him with wide eyes.

His gut turned sour. "I'm sorry, Ember. I didn't mean to be late." He couldn't tell how much she had heard. He wanted to keep her separate from his problems. Maybe Huck was right about him. That thought flashed across his mind like furious lightning before he could stop it. Huck was wrong about him. He was better than Johnny.

"I'm ready to go if you are." He moved toward her, wanting to leave his father behind.

"Give him a chance," she said.

"Thank you, young lady."

"Shut it, Johnny." He turned to Ember. "You don't understand what's happening here. Let's just go."

"But he's right."

"Excuse me?" The wind left his lungs. This woman whom he hardly knew but had taken hold of his heart in some strange way, was going to tell him Johnny Alvarez was right? "You don't know the first thing about this man."

"I don't. And by the vein pulsing in your neck, I'm not sure I would want to. But he understands something very important about you."

"He doesn't know me." And he wouldn't get to know

him either. His father was a stranger to him. Johnny had seen to that. He could live with the consequences of abandoning his children.

"You have a big heart. You can't hide it. I saw that at the train station. Consider what he's asking. If he doesn't keep up his end of the bargain, you can throw him out. I'll help you. I'm sure Brad will too."

"Bradford Wilde. You're still friends with him." Johnny's comment wasn't a question. He and Brad had been friends in high school, but not the way they had become later—close like brothers.

He had fiercely envied Brad's relationship with Silas, and he had told Johnny, not long before he left them, that he should be more like Brad's dad. Johnny had hauled off and punched him in the jaw for saying it, then he left two days later.

"The Wildes are my family." He wanted the dig to do some damage, and it did by the flinch of Johnny's shoulders. So why didn't he feel any better?

"Raf, think about it. For me," Ember said.

"If I think about it, can we go?" He'd say anything to make this moment end and to forget that maybe some of his last words to his father were the reason he walked out the door.

"Yes," she said.

He turned back to his father. "I'll call Ax in the morning with my decision."

"Muchas gracias, hijo."

"I'm not your son anymore."

He grabbed Ember's hand and led her to the truck, opening the door for her. She stopped halfway inside and turned to him.

"You did the right thing," she said.

"I haven't said yes yet."

"You will." She placed a kiss on his cheek.

His face warmed up where her lips brushed his skin. "We'll see." He had promised himself a long time ago that he wouldn't allow Johnny to hurt him or his brothers again.

And if he gave in to Johnny's wishes and he let them down, what would be the price this time?

CHAPTER FIFTEEN

"Where are we going?" Ember turned in her seat to get a better look at Raf. His hands gripped the steering wheel hard enough his knuckles were white. He hadn't said a thing since they got in the truck and drove away.

Maybe she had been out of line telling him to give his father another chance, but the pain in Johnny's voice had weighed on her. She wasn't sure why. It wasn't as if she knew the man. She had never met him, and he may not be the best person—she had no way of knowing that —but the remorse had lined itself on his face. The sorrow had been real.

Only Raf couldn't see past his own anger. She understood how the dark cloak of indignation could stop the brightest light from penetrating it. If her father asked for help, would she be able to give it? She doubted it.

Huck fought to be right even when he wasn't. He had never apologized for anything that she had been aware of. Johnny may have taken a long time to utter the words to Raf, but at least he had and that had been the nudge on her heart. She would give her left arm to hear her father say he was sorry.

"Raf?"

"Hmm?"

"Did you hear me?"

He straightened in the seat and shot her a wistful glance and a half smile. "I'm sorry. I was thinking. What did you say?"

"Do you want to reschedule? I know you have a lot on your mind. We can do this dinner thing another time." This whole thing was crazy. They were rushing things. Neither one of them was in a place to start a relationship. She should make him pull over and drop her off somewhere.

"No way. I won't let Johnny ruin our night. I'm just sorry you had to see it."

"I need to say something."

"Oh boy, this sounds serious."

"It is. If we're going to try each other on and see if we fit—at least while I'm in town as I have no illusions about a long-term thing—I need to know why you would want to get involved with me, knowing my father will always give you a bad time. He isn't going to come around. He isn't going to see the light. He won't say the right thing or do the right thing. It isn't in his makeup. My sisters and I are not more screwed up than we are because of our mother and now she's a memory of herself. Why do you want to be a part of any of that?"

"The tough questions right out of the gate." He turned onto a long driveway. The sign at the entrance read: Sunnyside Up Farm – No chickens here.

"You're taking me to a farm." The sign had thrown her. She wasn't expecting a farm for their date. She wasn't even dressed properly for an outdoor adventure of any kind.

"I am." He parked by the barn. "But before we get out, I want to answer you."

"Okay. Thank you for bringing the conversation back around."

He shifted to face her. "Huck doesn't scare me. Maybe he should. Maybe I should turn the truck right around and bring you back. Maybe I've lost my mind wanting to kiss Huck's daughter because he could end up trying to put a bullet in my head. But when I see you, all I want to do is taste you. If you can't handle the trouble your father is going to give us, then say so now. Because I want to do more than just kiss."

His smoldering gaze held her in place. Her mouth dried out, and her thighs trembled. The heat in the truck sent a trickle of sweat between her breasts.

"That was direct." And she liked it.

"I don't know how to say it any other way. Tell me. Can you handle your father?"

She had been handling her father her entire life. The difference now was she needed him on her side because of her mom. He had final say on her care. If he refused to bring in help, then she would have a big fight on her hands. Did she really want another fight over the man she was getting involved with?

But God help her, she didn't want to give up this chance for a moment of happiness. Raf shook loose things she had closed off and sealed away. She wanted to know what his lips against her body would do to her.

What would it be like to have his muscles pressed against her? She wanted to know what his hips would feel like with her legs wrapped around them.

She wasn't sure if she believed in soul mates, but the attraction to Raf was so fast and furious, she had to reconsider that theory. She pushed open the door and hopped out, hoping that was answer enough.

He hurried after her, taking her hand in his. The warmth of his skin comforted her, but he wasn't through. He gave a tug and pulled her against him.

His hand cupped her face. His strong jawline was dotted with the day's beard growth. She forced her hands to stop at his instead of reaching the rest of the way and running her fingertips along his jaw to see if it would scratch.

"Ember, I have one more request."

"What is it?" She would say yes to just about anything at the moment if only to feel his hands all over her.

"No games. We're always truthful with each other. No matter what. Are you prepared for your father to be against us?"

She should walk away—walk all the way back to the train station and ride until she was far away from Candlewood Falls. She doubted she would be much good here. "Don't worry about my father. I can handle him."

That wasn't a complete truth. She would try to handle Huck, but she had never mastered the art of dealing with him. Nyx was much better at that than she ever was. It would be best to say nothing to Huck about Raf and her. At least until she had figured out what was happening with her mom. After she was certain her mother's care had been upped, and her father was on board with that, then she would dance around the idea of her and Raf.

He placed a quick kiss on her lips and grabbed her hand again. "Good. Now come on. Dinner awaits."

She pushed the disappointment away. She would rather have him stand by the barn kissing her all night than dinner. Food wasn't on the list of her priorities at the moment.

"You brought me to the alpaca farm. I don't think I've ever been here. Isn't that crazy since my cousins' grandmother owns it?"

"Your cousin owns it now. Brooklyn bought it last fall. Cordy moved to Arizona." He guided her to a picnic table situated under an old oak tree.

White lights snaked up the trunk and over some of the low-lying branches. On the center of the table was a large mason jar with more white lights inside it, glowing as if the most brilliant of fireflies had been caught just for her.

The table was covered in a lace tablecloth and set for two. A picnic basket perched on the end. Nearby, a heat lamp glowed red. Raf had thought of everything. Maybe with a little help from Brooklyn, but she didn't care if the entire town had helped him. All of this was for her.

"This place is adorable. Is Brooklyn here?" Three alpacas roamed around on the other side of a wooden fence that connected to the barn and kept the alpacas separate.

"Actually, no. I asked her if I could have the place for just us. She doesn't normally do that, but—"

"But you have an in."

"I do." He flashed his bright smile. "Come say hello to the alpacas. The tan one is Alpacino. That guy there with the black fur is Chewpaca, and the two-toned one is Alistair. He's the resident crime stopper."

"What does that mean?"

"A story for another day. Brooklyn has two females, but they are in their side of the barn. I'm surprised Lucy hasn't come out to see what's going on. She's a natural alarm system."

"They sound like fun."

"They are. You should come back when Brooklyn is here and spend some time with them."

"I might like that. When we were kids, I only ever saw her and Brad at holidays and special events. The family usually avoided us because of my father."

"Even Silas? Silas seems as close as anyone can be to Huck." He pulled out sandwiches wrapped in white wax paper and handed her one.

"Uncle Silas would come around sometimes, but he was usually alone. I'm sure my father made Brad and Brooklyn uncomfortable."

"I think Brad's the one who makes your father uncomfortable now." He scooped potato salad that looked homemade onto their plates.

"Turnabout is fair play, I guess." Many times in her life she wondered what it would be like to have a father that people looked up to, admired even.

He brought his plate around and sat beside her. "I hope you don't mind, but it's warmer under the lamp."

She inched closer so their thighs touched. "Tell me about your family."

"Nothing much to tell. I have three younger brothers." He opened the iced tea and poured some into the glasses. "I didn't bring any wine or beer because I wasn't sure what you liked."

"Tell me something I don't know." She wasn't hungry. Her stomach had twisted into braids the minute he sat beside her. Her thoughts had swarmed to the things they could be doing to each other instead of sharing a meal. She should slow down. Food could be very sexual and used to entice what would happen next.

"We go camping together every summer. Sometimes Brad comes along. He likes the guy time since he doesn't have a brother and all his local cousins are women, except for Sam. And Sam isn't into roughing it."

"Do you miss your mom?" She already missed hers. Tomorrow she would get to the house early. She wanted another hand at a recipe or two. If her father still had the copier in his office at the house, she would make copies of the recipes to take with her.

"I hardly remember her." He leaned over and pulled out two slices of chocolate cake in a clear plastic container from the basket. "I brought dessert too."

A swift change in subject. She twisted the napkin, trying to find a way to say what she wanted. "If I ask you a question, will you answer it truthfully?"

"Always."

"Why don't you want to talk about your family and your past?"

He took her hand in his and ran his thumb over the top of her knuckles. Her skin tingled from his touch. "My past isn't made up of nice memories like most people's. There are no days at the beach or picnics at the park. I did what I had to in order to survive. I don't like to talk about it, okay?"

She wasn't sure if it was okay, but she wouldn't push for now. She and Raf were still new. There might be time for a deeper conversation, or she may be long gone and then what difference would it have made, knowing about his past. But she was curious and wanted to know what made him tick.

"What about other women?" If he wouldn't talk about his parents, maybe he'd spill a little about the kind of woman who had turned his head.

"What about them?"

"Is your past love life off-limits too?" She couldn't let him skirt every topic. If he asked, she would tell him some things about Keith.

"Why would you want to hear about another woman?" He squeezed her thigh.

"So I know what turns you off."

"You can find that out all by yourself. When something's not working, I'll tell you." He brushed his lips along her neck.

"Were you ever married? Can I at least ask that?" Her words came out in one long breath. Thoughts of his past relationships were quickly being dislodged by the expert performance of his lips by her earlobe.

"Never married. Never engaged. Good enough?" His breath was warm and sent shivers over her.

"But why?" She tangled her fingers in his hair, pressing him against her more.

"Because I hadn't met you yet."

CHAPTER SIXTEEN

Raf wanted to pack up the picnic, get the hell off the farm, and take Ember back to his place. He wasn't hungry for anything but her. Her lips tasted sweet and cool like the iced tea. He imagined the rest of her would be just as provocative.

He couldn't undress her and make love to her on the table, at least not at the farm. He didn't think the alpacas would notice, but Brooklyn and Caleb would be back soon. He couldn't embarrass them with his inability to control himself—again.

With regret, he eased out of the embrace. "Do you want to take this party someplace else?"

She leaned her forehead against his. "I hope you mean your house."

"In fact, I did." He didn't hesitate, but jumped up and started putting food and drinks back in the basket without regard for how he stacked things. He folded the tablecloth and turned off the lamp.

"See you guys," he said to the alpacas and grabbed Ember's hand.

He hurried through the streets of Candlewood Falls, hoping no one would pull him over. He didn't want anything to kill the mood. She was quiet during the ride, but she hadn't removed her hand from his. He would take that as a good sign that she wasn't having second thoughts.

The front of the truck dipped as he swung into the driveway, causing them to bounce in their seats. He should get the driveway fixed. But not tonight. Tonight he had much more important matters to contend with. He would have a smart and sexy woman in his bed in about five minutes. He hit the brakes a little too hard as he pictured Ember beneath him. "Sorry about the driving." He threw the truck in park.

Her smile spread slow and wide, like an anticipated gift.

"I hadn't noticed," she said.

At the front door, he fumbled with his keys, dropping them. Her laughter filled the air like a soap bubble. He kissed her instead of grabbing the keys because he couldn't wait to be inside.

Her soft curves fit against him as if they were pieces of the same puzzle. He cupped her bottom and pulled her closer so she could see the effect she caused. A moan slipped from her lips, and his head spun.

Their tongues were a game of follow the leader. She tugged at the end of his shirt until she had access to his abdomen. The cool night air against his skin did nothing to squelch the heat within him. Her touch was like the afternoon sun coming out from behind the clouds. If they didn't open the door soon, he might take her right on the porch.

"Shit, Ember. We need to go in before the neighbors start taking pictures."

"Where did you drop the keys?" Her chest heaved against his.

He pulled away and resurrected the keys with a triumphant wave. Except when he put the key in the door, the knob gave way under his touch. "It's not locked."

"I might have forgotten to lock it when I came out. I had heard your raised voice and wanted to see what was going on. I'm sorry."

"It's okay. It's a good neighborhood." And if he had been robbed, so be it. As long as they left the bed.

He pushed open the door and let her go ahead of him. She had also left the lights on in the living room and kitchen. Also not a problem. He had no plans to be in those rooms, unless she wanted to.

She stopped in her tracks, sucking in a loud breath and he came up short behind her.

"What the hell?" he said over her shoulder to the intruder. Now he knew why all the lights were on.

"Hey, bro. I'm home." Tino held up a beer in salute, a grimace smeared across his face.

He dodged around Ember so he was standing between her and Tino. He hadn't seen Tino in over a week. Hadn't heard a word from him since he destroyed his house. He wanted to punch his brother in the face and hug him at the same time.

"What are you doing here?" And Tino had better have an explanation this time.

"I tried to go back to my place, but the locks were changed. When I came next door to talk to you, your door was open. You weren't home. So I thought I'd wait." He shrugged as if that was all the explanation that was needed.

"We have a lot to talk about, Tino, but not tonight. Tonight, get the hell out of my house."

"Who's your friend?" Tino said, not moving from his spot.

He hesitated. He didn't want Tino to know about Ember in any way. But he was too slow.

She stepped around him with her hand out. "I'm Ember."

Tino slipped his hand into Ember's and that greasy smile slipped wider. "Tino. Raf's brother that he treats like a baby."

"You don't look like a baby." She pulled away and stood beside him now. Her hand rested on his elbow. If she were trying to let Tino know where her allegiances stood, he was glad.

"I meant that I'm the youngest by a lot. It's nice to meet you, Ember."

"You need to leave." He wanted this conversation over. The mood between him and Ember might be over too.

"I'm sorry, Raf. I am. I freaked. It's no excuse, but I did. Let me pay for the damage I did. I have some cash." Tino dug his wallet out of the front pocket of his jeans.

"I don't want your money because who knows where it came from." For all he knew, Tino wanted to pay him with the money he stole from the orchard. He wasn't sure if he could ever trust Tino again. So much hurt spread between them.

"I got some work. Some mechanic stuff. It paid pretty well," Tino said.

"Did you steal the money like you stole from the orchard?" That wasn't the right way to handle this. He had been afraid that something terrible had happened. Now that Tino stood in his house, completely fine, his insides shook with anger.

"I shouldn't have done that. I made a mistake."

"It's a mistake because you got caught. If Huck hadn't figured out that you were lying about the customers' orders and taking the money they paid us, you'd still be doing it."

"My father figured it out?" Ember gripped his arm harder.

He couldn't meet her gaze. Would she think worse of his family because Huck had been directly involved?

"Yeah. He caught Tino." Anger swirled with disgust. He had raised Tino better than that. He knew he had, and Tino hadn't learned a damn thing watching him go to work every day or making his lunch or talking to his teachers. He had devoted his entire damn life to Tino and all the thanks he got was a kick to the face.

"Please, let me pay for what I did."

"I don't believe you're suddenly so remorseful. Something else is going on. What happened to this mechanic's job you secured?"

Tino dropped his gaze and toed the floor with the edge of his shoe as if he were still five.

"Tino? Answer me. What did you do now?"

Tino's head snapped up. His gaze burned with fury. "Why do you always assume I did something wrong?"

"Because you usually do."

"It wasn't my fault. The guy that owned the garage accused me of doing something I didn't do. It was the other guy, but he blamed me." Tino fisted his hands at his sides.

"It's never your fault. I don't want your money. I wanted your respect because after all I've done for you, you repaid me by trashing my house. Why would you do that?" He wanted the pain in his gut to go away. Instead, it climbed up his throat, threatening to choke him.

"Can we talk outside? You know... just us." Tino tilted his head toward Ember.

"You know what, we're not talking at all. You can explain yourself another time. And it's not your apartment anymore. I rented it."

Ember shot him a questioning look.

"To who?" Tino put the beer down on the counter with some force. The bottle rattled against the marble.

"None of your business. Now go because I can't look at you." He turned his gaze away from Tino before he said or did something else he regretted. Like telling him that he had rented the apartment to Johnny. Which would drive Tino mad. And he would deserve it, too.

Heavy footsteps pounded the floor. The door closed with a click. The fight drained from him like a river spilling into a lake and he sank down on the sofa with a heavy sigh.

Ember sat beside him and took his hand. "I'm sorry."

"Do you see why I don't want to talk about my family?" He tilted his head back and let his skull sink into the pillow.

"Is there anything I can do to help?" She squeezed his hand.

"Would you mind turning out some of the lights? I think I'd prefer to sit in the dark."

"Would you also prefer to sit alone?" She pushed off the sofa. As the lights extinguished, the level of pain in his head dropped with each one.

"I might not be good company." He shouldn't allow Tino to ruin the night, but seeing his smug brother sitting in his house as if nothing had happened between them had sent the fire through his veins.

It had taken all his resolve not to shake Tino, especially when he had soaked up Ember as if he might eat her. Tino was so much like Johnny. That was the thing that had kept him up at night through the years. Tino had that mean streak deep and long.

He stood and took Ember's hand. "Come with me."

"Where are we going?" She stumbled after him. "Raf, slow down. I'm not exactly in my running shoes."

"Sorry." He tried to drop his pace, but he suddenly had the urge to get out of the house. He wanted to recapture what they had started at the farm.

He took her across the yard to the shed he had built a few years ago. Brad and Silas had helped him. Silas had all the building experience because he had built his cabin. Brad's brawn was good for carting and carrying, but Brad had a lot of his father's instincts. Sometimes he was jealous of Brad and all the good things his life was full of. And right after that he would admonish himself. His life hadn't turned out so badly considering where it had started. But still, he often wondered what it would have been like to have a father who taught him to build things like a house and grow things like an orchard.

"You want to show me your shed?" Ember coasted to a stop beside him.

"It's what's inside." He inserted a key into the lock and turned until the shackle popped. He had never brought a woman back here and had never shared with one what he did inside even before he had a shed to do it in.

He pulled the string and the row of lightbulbs in the ceiling cast their glow. He also turned on the table lamp in the corner where he kept all his carving tools organized.

"What is all this?" Ember moved slowly around the room, running her fingers along the worktable and the shelves where he kept the pieces he had finished.

"I like to carve wood." He also loved the smell of wood when it breathed its life into the air. But the wood he used to carve with had no distinguishing smell. Maybe it did when it was still in tree form. He'd have to find out someday.

"I can see that. You've made a forest full of animals." She picked up the owl and turned it in her hands.

Something warm filled his chest and puffed it up with its weight. "It's a hobby."

"Looks a little more like an obsession. These chess pieces are really cool." She pointed to the shelf where he kept the completed chess pieces he had created. He still had more to go, but he was in no rush.

"Thanks. I started making animals and spinning tops when I was about twenty. I needed a way to relax that wouldn't wake Tino after he went to bed." He had lived with his brothers and Johnny in a two-bedroom modular house on the outskirts of town where anyone who couldn't afford to live anywhere else took up camp like vagabonds.

His mother was gone by then. His father had shown him how to whittle when he was twelve. He had soaked up the time with his father like a dried-out sponge.

The skill had come in handy over the years, and his hobby had grown with him. He learned to make things like a walking stick and a life-size lion's head.

She examined the knight. "How do you make something like this?"

"I like smaller-sized basswood for the chess pieces. I draw a stencil onto the wood on all four sides. Then with one of my knives, whichever I'm in the mood for, I carve. When I'm done, I sand it down. Not hard, really." His favorite tool was just a pocketknife he had picked up years ago. As he moved up the ladder at the orchard and he could afford to, he purchased the expensive knives he had hanging on the wall.

"Would you make me something?" The blues of her eyes darkened and a smile played against her lips.

"What would you like?" He moved closer to her as if some other force controlled him.

"I've always been partial to bunnies. I wanted one as a kid, but I wasn't allowed to have one. Can you make a bunny?" She wrapped her arms around his neck and teased him by swaying her hips.

"I'll see what I can do." He would carve an entire colony of bunnies for her if it meant she'd continue to do what she was doing.

"You could sell these, you know."

"I don't think so."

"There has to be a market for this stuff. You could make a fortune, I bet."

"I don't need a fortune. Besides, I have a job." And he didn't want to waste time thinking about his employment. Coming out to the shed had worked its magic on him, and he was back in that space with Ember before Tino had shown up. All he wanted to think about was her.

She eased out of the embrace and leaned against the counter. Her absence was like a howling, cold wind ripping through his clothing.

"Do you like working at the orchard?" she said.

"Is that what you want to talk about?" He would much rather take this conversation inside. Maybe light a fire and undress her in the light of the flames. Talking optional.

"Just answer the question. I'm curious."

He grabbed the stool and dropped down. If this was what she wanted... "It's the only job I've had for the past twenty-three years."

"That's not what I asked. My father loves the orchard. He would rather be there than anywhere else. I would guess my Uncle Silas does too because he's still there. What little I know about Brad says dirt is in his blood. But you, do you like working there?"

He opened his mouth to say of course he did. That the Wildes were his family and that place meant as much to him as it did to them. But for some reason he swallowed back the words.

"Then why do you stay?" She shoved off the counter and came to him, placing her hands on his chest.

Relief washed over him like water from a hot bath. He took her hands and wrapped her arms around his neck so she would be up against him—the place she belonged. But now he had a question of his own. "Why did you leave your job?"

"Because I never wanted to be in the technology field. I've always hated it. I only went in that direction because of my father. He wanted all of us to have careers we could rely on. I was wrong to listen."

"What do you want to do now?"

"Right now, I want you to kiss me, then take me inside and make love to me. The rest I'll figure out later."

A low whistle passed through his teeth. "The lady's wish is my command."

And he kissed her.

CHAPTER SEVENTEEN

E mber couldn't remember how she and Raf got across the yard and up to his bedroom, but they had. She had a few glimpses of stopping along the way to kiss and remove a piece of clothing until they were in the kitchen in their underwear. She was pretty sure her jeans were still in the yard. The last few steps to the foot of his bed were a blur of touching and hurrying, and him tripping over the last step.

His hands were on her now, setting her on fire, which was good because five minutes ago, standing in the kitchen, the tile floor had nipped at her toes and before that the chilly night air had coated her skin.

But here in his room that smelled like lemon polish and a masculine undertone of bergamot, she was warm and safe.

She tilted her head back to give him more access to her neck. He bent her backward, supporting her with his strong arms as he kissed her throat and then her collarbone. He left a trail down her breasts, but he stopped before going any further. She bit back a curse, not wanting him to cease the delicious teasing even if it was driving her mad.

His skilled mouth transported her to new heights. Making love had never been like this, where every touch demanded more. She tangled her fingers in his silky hair and held his mouth against her breast as if she were holding on to the crumbling edge of a river bank threatening to dump her in the rapids.

He scooped her up and delivered her to the bed, sliding in beside her. He brushed the hair away from her face with a tender touch. "You are the most beautiful woman I have ever seen."

"Thank you." She ran her fingers across his jaw and to her delight, his stubble scratched against her skin. "You're beautiful too." And he was with his long legs and toned body.

His chest hair was like down under her touch. His hips were thin and solid. His skin was soft, except for his hands. Those were calloused from hard work, but she loved their rough feel. He was the perfect male and with a caring heart on top of it all.

He kissed her again, long, hard, and deep. Wanting to memorize every inch, her hands wandered until she had the full length of him. A deep guttural sound escaped from his lips and satisfied her.

But he returned the favor when his hands left her torso and dipped lower, finding her center. His finger was inside her, coaxing her to her zenith. With his other hand, he pushed hers away from touching him. "You first," he whispered against her ear.

Her body gave in to his encouraging caresses, and

she wondered for a brief moment where he had learned to seduce a woman. She knew so little about him, but tonight, she was glad she had rushed into this thing with him.

She gripped his arm as he brought her closer to the edge, but he pulled away before she could fall over. The mounting pressure between her legs from every stroke was wonderfully incredible and still not enough. She wanted more and reached for him again. "I need all of you."

He gave her his high-voltage smile and settled between her legs. The heat of him near her scorched her. With one thrust he was inside her, and her hips pushed up to meet his. He took control of the pace, slow at first, but then with more urgency as he responded to her sounds.

"Can we switch?" The words had popped into her head like a giant neon sign and then shot out of her mouth.

He hesitated. "Is something wrong?"

"God, no. It's incredible. I just wanted to see what it felt like to be on top."

He barked out a loud laugh. "Of course you do." In one swift move, he flipped them so she was lying on top of him.

That high-voltage smile took on a mischievous quality. He raised his hands above his head. "Have your way with me, then."

She pushed up so she was straddling him and took him in. He was the sexiest man she had ever been with. A piece of his black hair had fallen over his eye. That smile never wavered as if he were in the exact spot he was supposed to be. And she hoped so since she was on top of him, with him all the way inside her, their hips rocking.

She had complete control of the ride now and she didn't hesitate. She directed every movement so she could feel all of him colliding into the spot that desired him most. The movements became frantic. She clasped hands with his to pull herself down on him further and the spasms shook her from her roots to her toes.

He flipped her again before she could catch her breath and thrust inside her until he stilled and shuddered. He collapsed against her, kissing her neck.

She wrapped her arms around him, pulling him close as their breathing calmed and their hearts slowed. She may never want to leave this bed or this man.

And she would have to if her past couldn't exist with her future.

Raf eased out of bed and shoved his legs into his boxers. The room was cold and the moon cast its white glow through the windows, giving him enough light to find a sweatshirt and some jeans. Ember slept curled up under the sheet. He pulled the blanket around her.

He watched her for a second. The line between her brows had smoothed out. A hint of a smile tugged at her lips. He hoped she was dreaming about the night they just had. He would be for a long time to come.

Closing the door behind him with a gentle click, he wandered downstairs. He had told her he wasn't much of a television watcher. He also wasn't much of a sleeper.

Not that he had minded being tangled up with her. He could make love to her all night, but after round two they had dozed off for a while. Now, he would probably be up for the rest of the day. No complaints. If getting up at three every morning meant he went to bed with Ember the night before, he would consider himself lucky.

He wiped a hand over his face and put on a pot of coffee. He needed to figure out what to do about Tino's return and Johnny wanting to move in next door. He also needed to figure out what he was going to do about the beautiful woman in his bed whose father would want to kill him when he found out.

"You got yourself in a pretty good mess this time, Rafael," he said to the empty room.

He shouldn't want to be involved with someone whose father couldn't accept him. Hadn't he spent most of his life trying to find the place he fit in? Wasn't that why the orchard and the Wildes—Brad and Silas, and sure, Brooklyn too—were so important to him? They had accepted him right from the start. No questions asked.

Ember had said she could handle her father, but he wondered. Was running out of town her idea of handling Huck? She had taken on a career because Huck had told her to. What was really in her heart? Did she even know?

"Shut up, Alvarez. You're going to blow the best thing to walk through your door in a long time." He grabbed a mug from the cabinet. He really needed to stop talking to himself.

A thud hit the porch, almost like someone dropping off a delivery. But there were no deliveries at this hour. If

Tino had come back... He hurried to the window and peered around the curtain.

"Raf?"

He swung around. Ember stood in the soft glow of an accent light in the kitchen. Her hair was messed, and she had a crease on her cheek. But she looked beautiful wearing his t-shirt that hung to her knees.

"Hey. Someone's outside. Go back upstairs, okay?" He kept his voice at a whisper.

"Like hell I will." She did not lower her voice. Why did he think she would?

"Ember, please. I don't know what's out there. I don't want you getting hurt." He would never forgive himself if something happened to her, and neither would Huck.

"I can take care of myself. And besides, I want to help you."

"I know you can take care of yourself, and I appreciate the help, but when was the last time you got into a fistfight?" He didn't wait for an answer because he wasn't expecting one. "You work and live in a safe world. I've been in my share of fights and can drag a tree if I need to. I would prefer to handle this myself."

She marched right up to him as if he hadn't spoken. "Let me see what's out there."

He didn't budge. "What are you going to do?" This stubborn woman would be the end of him.

"Open the door and look out." She fisted her hands on her hips.

"And what if there's an intruder? Do you think you're going to fight him off in your magical t-shirt? 'Cause I'm pretty sure you don't have a weapon under that thing." He knew exactly what was under there, and he didn't want anyone else seeing it.

"Magical t-shirt? What are you talking about? Foolish man. There's no intruder. If there were, we wouldn't be sitting here talking about it. They'd already be inside the house. Could it just be your brother?"

"I have no doubt that it's Tino trying to break in so he can have a place to sleep. Which means he's probably drunk. I don't want you to see that."

"I won't judge you by your brother, if that's what you're worried about."

A fierce, quick knock interrupted them. He nearly jumped out of his skin.

She waved a hand as if to say, go ahead open it. He put his back to her because no matter what the independent lady said, he wanted to keep her safe. And opened the door.

"Ax?" His brother stood on the porch with his hair sticking up in all directions. His hooded eyes were bloodshot.

"Sorry to wake you." Ax pointed to the porch where a passed-out Tino lay.

"What happened?" He went outside and closed the door before Ember could follow him. He also didn't want Ax seeing Ember in his shirt and making all kinds of conclusions—which would be right because Ax wasn't stupid.

"The dumb shit was at Murphy's tying a few on. He drunk-dialed Matt. That went badly. Matt tried to call you, but you didn't answer." Ax raised his brows and smirked. He must've seen Ember anyway. "Then Matt called me and here we are. I didn't know where to take him."

"I don't want him."

"He can't stay with me. I already have Johnny. That's enough Alvarez drama. Matt told me he'd cut my balls off if I dropped Tino at his place. Not that I want to drive an hour to the shore."

"It's three a.m. Murphy's closed at two. Where have you been for the last hour?"

"Waiting for Tino to finish vomiting in the bushes. It's been a shitty night, Raf. I'm working on a commission for my next show. I need some sleep. I don't care if he spends the night on the porch. But can he stay here?"

"What about Johnny?"

"What about him? I'm waiting for you to tell me if he can rent this place." Ax gave out a giant-size yawn.

"And then have the two of them living here? You're out of your mind, Axel. You keep one. I'll keep one." He didn't want Ax to bear Tino's burden, that was his job, but he couldn't handle both his father and his brother.

"So, you'll let Johnny move in here?" Ax's eyes grew wide with hope.

"Does that mean you'll take Tino?" He might be able to keep his distance from Johnny easier than Tino. Tino would be knocking on his door all the time, which he did not want while Ember lived with him.

"After my latest show, I need the space and the quiet to work. My work isn't like yours. The interruptions kill my creativity."

"Oh, for fuck's sake. You spray paint." That wasn't fair and he knew it.

"I create, motherfucker. Don't ever forget it." Ax

shoved him and laughed just like when they were kids and Ax would only pretend to be upset over something Raf had done. Ax's ability to let the bad things go was a gift—a gift Raf wished he possessed.

"I don't want them both here." He had to stand firm on that much.

"Johnny promises to keep an eye on Tino. Let them both do the work. Johnny also said he can get Tino a job with his union. Right after my show, I swear, I'll let one of them move back in."

"Unless one of them kills the other first. Or me."

"Either way, the problem is solved." Ax burst out laughing.

He smacked Ax in the head.

"Hey." Axel swung back, but he ducked just in time to miss the collision.

"Still too slow, little brother."

"Who's the woman? It's Ember Wilde, isn't it?" Ax shoved his hands in the pockets of his hoodie, expertly changing the subject.

"Forget what you saw." He could also change subjects when the topic didn't suit him.

"Yeah, right. I saw an attractive woman standing behind you in the middle of the night, clearly wearing your shirt. No one would forget that. You're getting it on with Huck Wilde's daughter. You are crazy."

"Don't say anything to anybody. Especially not this one." He pointed to a snoring Tino. "Or Johnny. We don't want Huck to know the extent of things just yet." He could trust Ax to keep his secrets. It was Tino who couldn't be trusted.

"You want to keep a secret in this town? Good luck."

"Brad Wilde kept a secret for ten years."

"Yeah, well, you're not Brad. Are you going to leave Tino out here?"

"Help me bring him inside the apartment. He can sleep on the floor." They hefted Tino to a standing position while Raf unlocked the door. They made it to the couch, where they dropped Tino on his side.

"Thanks," Ax said.

"Don't thank me yet. I have a feeling trouble is on the horizon."

CHAPTER EIGHTEEN

E mber let herself into her parents' house. She had waited down the street until she saw her father drive away for work. She wasn't ready to see him. He would be able to take one look at her and know what she and Raf had done last night. He could always tell when she or her sisters had done something they didn't want him to know about. It was probably her inability to make eye contact or the hot blush that crept up her neck and stained her cheeks. And every memory of her and Raf in bed had heat flushing her face.

"Anybody home?" she called out so as not to frighten her mother who must be somewhere in the rambling house that felt too large for just her parents.

For years, she wondered if they would downsize after each daughter packed her bags for the last time. But every year that passed told a different story. Her parents were there to stay as the empty rooms echoed with silence and the pages on the calendar fell. Knowing her father and his ability to split a penny in two, the house was probably paid for. The cost wouldn't be the issue. But what did it feel like to move from room to room where there was once life and now there were only shadows of better times? And were they even better? She had never bothered to ask.

"Who's there?" Mom said from somewhere inside the house.

"Mom, it's Ember." She ducked into the kitchen. The room smelled of burnt toast and coffee. The breakfast dishes were piled on the side of the sink and the vinyl tablecloth was covered in crumbs and what might be jelly.

Mom always straightened the house or performed some kind of chore right after she and her sisters had left for school. If Mom was falling back into old routines, like her trip to the park, she could be gliding around the house with a duster in her hand. That image was more palatable than her mother wandering the streets aimlessly.

Only Mom wasn't dusting. She sat at the dining room table staring at the fragments of a jigsaw puzzle. She lifted her head at the creak in the floorboards and smiled. Her mother always had a smile whenever she walked into a room. No matter what Mom was doing, she would turn at the sound of one of her children entering and light the world on fire with her smile.

"Hello, dear. What brings you by?" Mom returned to the task of finding a piece to fit. She clapped with enthusiasm at her discovery.

Tears sprung up like a hose that burst a hole. She swatted them away and took a breath to keep the emotion out of her voice. "I wanted to see how you were feeling today."

"I'm fine. Why wouldn't I be?"

Why indeed? She pulled out the chair next to her mom. "When did you start doing jigsaw puzzles?" Puzzles helped the brain activity of people with Mom's condition. "Did Petra bring this for you?"

"Petra? Don't be silly. Petra doesn't have time to run over here with games for me. Your father bought it off the line."

"Off the line? Do you mean online?"

"From the computer. You know I'm not a fan of computers. But your father is a whiz." Mom secured another piece in the puzzle.

She had a hard time picturing her father as some kind of computer guru, but if she were being honest, he was a smart man who helped run a very successful business. There wasn't any reason why he wouldn't have taught himself how to navigate technology. Sometimes it was hard for her to give him credit for anything. That wasn't always fair. She did have a few good memories of her childhood that included him. "That was nice of him to get you a puzzle."

"He's been reading about my situation," she leaned in and whispered as if the china cabinet might overhear them and tell her secrets to the plates collecting dust inside it.

"Mom, if things get worse, does Dad know what you want?"

Mom stared at her with watery eyes. "Things will get worse. Much worse. Your father will know what to do. He always does." Mom pushed out of the chair. "Goodness, we've been sitting here a while. My leg fell asleep. I think I'd like to have some tea and move outside for some fresh air."

"Mom, we should talk about your care." She stood too.

"No, Ember, dear. There is nothing to talk about."

"But Mom—"

Her mom put a hand up. "Stop. Today is a good day. I don't want to think about tomorrow. I want to enjoy today, doing my puzzle and spending time with my daughter. I know you came back to town for me. I wish you wouldn't have done that because you have a life to live, but it's nice to have you around."

"But not in the house."

"You were always the sensitive one. It's such a wonderful quality to feel the pain of others and take care with them, but such a burden to feel your own pain so intensely. It doesn't seem you can have one without the other. Anyway, it's better for everyone that you have your own space. Children need their own space, even when they're small, and especially when they're grown."

"Why does it feel like you're pushing me away?"

Mom placed a chilled hand on her cheek. "My sweet, sweet Ember. You don't need to take care of me. Take care of yourself."

"What do you mean? I'm taking care of myself just fine." Her mother could still see right through her. Her self-care had been nonexistent for some time. She had been dragging herself to a job she didn't like because she hadn't had the courage to leave it. She had stayed in a relationship with a man who hadn't been suited for her for the same reasons.

"Why are you really home?"

"To help you. Mom, we need to talk about your care. Your wishes." All of it. She wanted to talk about the past and write down all the memories so she wouldn't lose her mother entirely.

"We don't need to talk about any of that. If you would like some tea and to tell me how you're doing, please join me. If not, I'll see you later." Mom walked away without another word, leaving her reeling.

She refused to move, unsure of what to do next. She had returned home because Petra had said Mom couldn't remember. That she had been in line at the grocery store and couldn't recall the words she needed to pay the cashier. The cashier had thought Mom was having a stroke and called for help.

But she had also returned home because her life in the city was over. At forty-one, she needed to reinvent herself and she didn't know where or how to begin. Candlewood Falls had seemed like the best choice. Being somewhere familiar was like grabbing a buoy out at sea.

That choice had brought her to Raf, which she was glad for. He was an interesting man with a troubled past, but he was sweet and caring. A little overprotective, but deep down she relished him taking the lead. But what else would her return home bring? Could it help her fix the past?

Dishes clanked in the other room. She followed the sound to find her mother washing dishes and humming a tune. Her recipe book lay open on the counter.

"Were you planning on baking?" She ran her finger over the soft page.

"Hmm?" Mom turned. "Oh, I thought about it for a

minute, but I don't feel like tackling the work. Would you like to bake something? I should have all the ingredients."

"Maybe. Mom, I met someone." This might be her only chance to tell her about Raf. Even as soon as tomorrow, her mother could forget this moment. She and Raf might be over before they even start—she had no illusions—but if he were the one, she would want the chance to tell her mom about the man who finally won her heart.

"Someone you're interested in?" Mom put water in the teakettle and the kettle on the stove.

"I still can't believe it. It happened kind of quickly." Maybe for the first time, rushing in to things would pay off.

"Just like when I met your father." Mom opened the wooden box on the counter and dangled two tea bags from her fingers.

"You said it was at an event at the orchard."

"Oh, it was. I saw him standing at a booth where they were selling candied apples. He was so handsome and so young. Tall with dark hair. Those stunning blue eyes." Mom stared off in the distance as if she could travel back and be inside her memory.

"So, you knew from that moment that he was the one?" She wanted to ask, *but what happened when he opened his mouth and said those hurtful things about other people*, but she bit back the words. She wanted to remember her mother like this—happy, at peace.

"Not at all. I just knew he was probably the most handsome man I had ever seen. He was standing between Silas and SJ and even though there is a strong family resemblance, Huck had been the one to take my breath away. I couldn't stop myself. I had to speak with him."

"So you walked right up to him and bought an apple."

"You remember the story. I won't bore you with it again." Mom turned her back and grabbed the sugar bowl from the cabinet.

"Tell it, Mom. Tell me how Dad made you fall in love with him." She wanted to see another side to her father, a side kept from her.

"I'd rather hear about your young man. What's his name?"

She placed her hands flat on the counter to steady herself. "Rafael."

"The archangel of healing."

"What?"

"It's believed that Raphael was an angel who could heal. I read that somewhere." Her mother waved her hand in the air as if to wipe away the value of what she had said. "Anyway, it's a lovely name."

She didn't know about an angel named Raphael, but the meaning of his name fit him. He was trying to save his brother. And he had offered her a little healing too.

"He works at the orchard." Her mother would have to put the dots together. Her father had to have mentioned a man named Rafael that worked with him somewhere over the years. She must have set foot on the orchard and seen him. Or spoken to Brad or Silas, and Raf must have walked up. This was Candlewood Falls. Everyone knew everyone else.

"You've become involved with Raf Alvarez." Her

mother slumped against the counter. "I should have realized. Maybe I would have been quicker at one time."

"You know him, then?" She held her breath.

"We're not friends, if that's what you mean. He's worked there for decades. I've met him many times. He has a famous brother and a brother who is a lot of trouble. I think there might be one other one too. He raised them, didn't he?"

"He did. He's a good man. I think I really like him." Saying the words out loud was like a helium balloon floating in the sky.

"Is it serious?"

"Not yet. It may never be. I just wanted you to know I'm spending time with someone who makes me happy for now."

"And what happens when you leave town?"

"What if I don't?" She had considered staying, but not seriously until right now. Raf had given her a reason to stick around.

"Why would you stay?"

"To be with you." That was also part of it. She wanted to spend as much time with her mother as she could. She had allowed too much time to go by already.

"Don't waste your time on me, Ember."

"But Mom—" The teakettle whistled and interrupted her.

"I don't want to be a burden to anyone. That was never the plan. I especially don't want to be a burden to my children. Your father and I have things figured out. You don't have to concern yourself with that part of my life. You can go back to living yours."

"You are pushing me away." She was certain of it.

"I want your memories of me to be good ones. Or at least decent ones. Like today. I don't want you to remember me as someone who can't remember how to swallow." Tears filled her eyes, but her mom tilted up her chin, not letting one fall.

"I want to stay in town and help take care of you."

"No. I won't allow it. You wanted to know my wishes. That is it. You and your sisters are not to be my caregivers. If that's why you're in town, then leave town." Mom hurried from the room. Footsteps pounded the stairs.

The tea forgotten.

Without thinking, she grabbed the recipe book, tucking it under her arm. She let herself out, much the way she had let herself in. Unnoticed. She drove around town until she found a place to stop.

She turned onto the driveway and read the sign. Sunnyside Up Farm – No chickens here.

The sign helped her drive the rest of the way. She needed a place where there were no chickens because she had never been more frightened in her life. And not because she had stolen her mother's recipe book.

But because her mother had set her loose. She had come home only to care for her mother, or at the very least learn what her wishes were about her care.

Now she knew her mother wanted to live her life without her daughters in it. The pain from that cut in a way she didn't know existed. And that pain was what had her scared. The only other thing that rivaled that fear, was the fear of what losing Raf might do to her.

CHAPTER NINETEEN

Raf couldn't believe this was happening. How had he gotten roped into allowing Johnny to move into his apartment? He was a sucker for his younger brothers, that's how. When Ax had said he needed some time alone to work, he couldn't refuse to help. Ax deserved the space to focus on his work that mattered to so many people, and Raf couldn't be prouder. He had to give Ax the time he needed. And when Ax's show was over, he and Ax would help Johnny and Tino find other places to live. Preferably in a different town.

So, not only was Johnny carrying a packing box into the extra unit, but Tino followed Johnny inside just like he used to when they were kids. Not only Johnny, but Tino would be next door, only separated from him by a wall. And Ember was living with him. She had taken up space in the extra bedroom, but after last night, he hoped she'd just slip into his bed. Even though he liked her, maybe too much too soon, how the hell had his life twisted around so much?

"You know, you could offer to help," Tino said as he shifted the box in his arms and trotted up the porch steps.

"I am helping. I'm giving you a place to stay." And he had taken a day off work to make sure Tino and Johnny didn't get into it and cause more damage than there already was. Brad had shaken his head when he told him what was going on.

"Not for free," Tino said over his shoulder.

"I don't owe you any favors, Santino." He cupped his hands around his mouth to make sure his voice echoed off Tino's back. "You should be kissing my backside."

"Give him a break, hijo." Johnny stepped back onto the porch from inside the house and wiped his hands on his pants.

"Johnny, for the hundredth time, stop calling me that." The term of endearment reminded him of the few times Johnny had acted like a father, which had confused Raf as a child and made him think Johnny could be different.

Nothing was ever different with Johnny. He let them all down over and over. He didn't care what Johnny had said about changing. He would need to see some proof.

"But you are my son."

"In biology only." If he had a child, he would show up every day to show his kid how much he loved them. He wouldn't let them down. Leave them sitting on the school steps with no way home. He wouldn't throw things against the wall to stop himself from hitting his wife whose drug addiction was a constant battle.

"Then why allow me to stay here?"

"Because Ax needs help. And unlike you, I will do whatever it takes to help out my brothers."

"I wish you would stop holding such grudges." Johnny sat on the edge of the porch and patted the space beside him. He pulled out a pack of cigarettes from his shirt pocket and lit up.

He stood where he was. "We have a temporary arrangement. Ax needs some quiet while he works. You are going to fix up my place, and Tino is going to help you because it's his mess. After that, we go our separate ways." And that wouldn't be soon enough.

"Do you still whittle?" Johnny asked as if he hadn't said anything at all about their new living arrangement.

"We aren't friends, Johnny."

"I'm making a little small talk while I take a break. I'm not as young as I used to be." Johnny took a drag and blew smoke circles into the air.

"Stop smoking. You'll feel a hell of a lot better. Besides, you're not that old." His parents had him when they were only twenty. Too young to start a family. He had never asked, but he assumed the pregnancy came before the proposal had.

"Older than you. Enjoy the spring you still have in your step. And the fact your dick still gets up."

"Jesus, don't say stuff like that."

"Why not? You're a young man with a beautiful woman in your life." Johnny winked.

"What are you talking about?" A cold shiver ran over his skin. Johnny knowing about Ember wouldn't be good. And that would also mean Huck knowing couldn't be too far behind. Huck already hated the idea of Ember and him being together because of his ethnicity and because Tino had spent time in jail.

Johnny choked out a laugh. "I've been to town, Rafael. The people of Candlewood Falls still talk like they have no control of their tongues. You took a certain lady out on a date the other night. You were also seen kissing that same lady out in public."

"She's none of your business."

"Fine. Fine." Johnny sucked hard on his cigarette. "Let me say this. She's lucky to have you. You turned into a fine man. I knew you would be better off without me around. I was right. And you did right by your brothers. Better than I ever could have."

"Let me ask you something." He faced his father.

"Please. I will answer anything."

"If you thought we were so much better off without you, why did you stick around for eighteen years, causing all your trouble? Can you explain that to me?"

"I was a poor excuse for a man back then. It took landing in prison and rehab to set me straight. But I stayed because even with all my problems, I was better than your mother ever was. You couldn't be left alone with her. In no time at all, she would have lost custody of you four."

"Why did you have kids?"

"Your mother wanted someone to love. And when babies were around, she cleaned up for a while. After you were born, I thought we might have a chance at being a real family. I should have taken you and disappeared before Matias had arrived. By then, I was too far gone to care for you both all by myself. And I foolishly loved your mother."

So had he.

"Are you two going to sit on your asses all day?" Tino sauntered through the door with a scowl on his face.

"I'm not the one moving in." He'd had enough heart-to-hearts for the time being. He could go into work for a few hours, or he could find out where Ember was and see if she wanted to meet for a cup of coffee.

"Come on, Santino." Johnny pushed off the porch and grabbed Tino by the shoulder. "Let's get settled in. Tomorrow we start fixing the walls you damaged."

Tino shook off Johnny and stopped in front of him. "I am sorry, Raf, about the house. And about the last night when Ax dumped me here. I know I said it before, but I want to make sure you believe me. I won't do anything to hurt you again. I promise."

Tino had that big-eyed look he used to get as a kid when he got caught smoking weed in their apartment or when a teacher called home to say Tino hadn't been to class in a week. His heart said Tino, the baby of the family who needed so much attention, meant every word.

"You had better not. Or it will be the last time."

His head said something entirely different.

The tree line that bordered the alpaca farm burst with whites and pinks. Yellow leaves splashed over purples that were tucked into the browns of new bark. Spring in New Jersey was a carnival of colors. But the festive shades changed as quickly as a sparkler fizzling out on the Fourth of July. Soon the seasonal hues would give in to the bossier greens.

Ember hesitated near the car. She had come to the farm hoping the acres of land and vibrant tree line would bring her some peace. And because she and Raf had had such a good time on their date.

Anything but tranquility was happening here.

One of the alpacas with almost white fur ran in circles, screeching as if it might be in pain. An older couple, holding to-go cups, backed away from the loud animal. The man held his hands in the air, surrendering to who knew what. The woman tripped over something in the ground and fell on her butt. The contents in the cup crested through the air like a wave crashing into a jetty and spilled over her top. She yelled. The alpaca yelled louder. By the looks of the mess soaking through her clothing, that cup had been filled with coffee, hot chocolate at best.

It was like watching a television show. Brooklyn tried to help the woman, but the woman shoved her away. The man said something Ember couldn't hear, and Brooklyn backed off.

Another woman wearing a trench coat and overalls tucked into combat boots shouted something about a stupid alpaca getting stuck. Brooklyn handed her a pair of scissors. The combat boot-wearing woman turned and ran into the field. She had seen that woman before but couldn't place where. Then it hit her. Weezer River. Of course.

A tall man wearing black jeans and a matching t-shirt hobbled down the front steps of the house, holding a bandage to his head. Caleb Ransom, with a trickle of blood from his hairline to jawline, spoke to the couple. The woman thrusted her cup, most likely now empty, at him and marched off. He threw the cup down and stormed into the barn. Brooklyn went in after him.

She turned to go. Finding the calm she needed would have to happen elsewhere.

Someone grabbed her arm, startling her. "Ember? Is that you?"

This new woman, younger than her by at least a decade, tugged at her brown hair pulled back in a ponytail. Her face was free from makeup, showing off her creamy complexion and naturally pink lips. She smoothed her beige knit shirt—which wasn't wrinkled—with her palms. Her hands were free from jewelry and her fingernails short and well taken care of. If Ember had to guess, she'd say this woman was a model.

But this woman wasn't a model. Not at least that Ember had heard through the Wilde family grapevine. "Brielle. When did you come back to Candlewood Falls?"

She hadn't seen her cousin Brielle in too many years to mention. Huck and Brielle's father, Cooper, were not close. Growing up, she and her sisters were denied ample opportunities to connect with Brielle and her siblings because of their fathers' differences. The age gap—she had been right about the decade between them—didn't help either.

"I'm in town for a friend's wedding. I can't believe I bumped into you. It's great to see you." Brielle's smile brightened her face and splashed some color on her cheeks. If she weren't a model, she should be.

"Yeah, it's great to see you too. What a surprise." This trip had held plenty of those. That was for sure.

"How is your family? Are you married? Gosh, I have

so many questions." Those well-manicured hands tugged at the collar of her shirt.

"Everyone is fine. Not married. How about you?" She would steer the conversation away from all the holes in her life. Save that information for a day when maybe they could sit at the coffee shop and have no interruptions.

"Definitely not married."

Brooklyn and Caleb had not come out of the barn. Weezer was making a return with an alpaca by her side. From this angle, it appeared that she chatted away with the animal as if they were old friends. Another car came up the driveway. A family with three kids piled out.

"I didn't realize the farm was so busy today. Can you tell Brooklyn I stopped by? I'll text her later." She couldn't stay with all the commotion. That one alpaca was still carrying on. And she wasn't ready for the kind of questions guaranteed to surface when the past bumped into the present unexpectedly. A lengthy conversation like that would have to wait.

"You can't leave. I mean... I just found you. Brooklyn was going to bring out tea, right after they unstuck Alpacino from the fence. Why don't you join us? You can fill me in on all that you've been up to."

"Thanks, but I don't want to be a burden. Brooklyn has her hands full. And clearly, you are here to spend time with her. I don't want to intrude on that."

"Honestly, I'm not here to hang out with Brooklyn. Well, not technically anyway. I'm here for an event."

"With that family that just pulled up?"

"Not them. Or even that couple that was here before.

Ends up I'm the only one from my group that came here. The event was a bit of a flop."

"What happened to the other people in your group?" The question was off her tongue before she could stop it. She couldn't exactly make a getaway if she asked questions, but seeing Brielle again shook loose memories of her childhood and the occasional times Uncle Cooper visited with his family. Those were good memories.

They had been a family once. And she wanted that back. She didn't want to feel so alone any longer. Losing her mother might take a part of her away too. Being Ruby's daughter was the only part that was still clearly marked.

"They all went to the gun range. I tried. I really did. But one second in there with all that noise and the idea someone could get shot and maybe killed. I couldn't stay. I ran." Brielle covered her face with her hands.

"I take it you don't like guns."

"I don't like anything too risky or adventurous. There, I said it." Brielle threw her hands in the air. "Please don't tell anyone I said that out loud."

"Your secret is safe with me. But I don't understand. Sometimes being a little reckless has its advantages." Moving into Raf's place had been one of the most reckless things she had done in a long time.

"I don't think so."

"What are you afraid of?" The question echoed in her head like a gong. She could be asking herself the same thing. What was she really afraid of?

"I'd much rather write about peril than partake in it."

"You're a writer, then?"

"Romance. What do you do?"

She opened her mouth to give the usual boring answer, but stopped and stole a glance at her car where her mother's recipe book lay on the front seat. "I'm starting a new business. I'm a baker." The tension leaked from her chest. It was as if she could breathe for the first time in months.

"That's great. I'll have to try your stuff."

"I might not be ready for customers before you leave." Considering she hadn't even decided until this very second that she would attempt her own business. She had no idea how to even go about becoming a commercial baker or if her skills were even good enough. But the idea was out there, floating like a soap bubble. Now she needed to take care with it. "Can I give you a piece of unsolicited advice?"

"Are you going to tell me to take a chance? Grab life with both hands? That kind of thing? Because, believe me, if I could do that, I would have already. I didn't want to be the only one who couldn't fire a gun today. And there is an entire week of activities lined up that has me sick to my stomach. I have no idea how I'm going to handle those."

"I can't tell anyone to grab life with both hands because I haven't done a very good job of that myself lately. But I can tell you that my mom always says even when you're scared, do it anyway."

Her mother was living that right now. She had to be frightened out of her mind with her diagnosis. The future so uncertain she had no idea if and when it would show up. But Mom kept going. She was trying to be strong by carrying the burden of her illness for her daughters even when they wanted to help. Just like Mom wanted her children to know she loved them, they wanted their mom to know they loved her. After all the years of taking care of them, of being the person who met their needs when their father couldn't, it was their turn to take care of her. She hoped she could convince Mom to let her in a little.

Brielle stared off into the distance. "Aunt Ruby. She was always one of my favorite aunts. Thanks, Ember. And tell your mom thanks too. If I can't do it for myself, I'll try to be brave for her."

So would she. Without thinking, she grabbed Brielle in a hug. Brielle stiffened at first, but then gave in and hugged her back. "Keep in touch, okay? And I hope you have a nice time at the wedding."

"Thanks. And I will."

Her phone vibrated. She dug it out of her back pocket. Raf's name lit up the screen. "I have to take this. I'm sorry."

"I'll see you soon." Brielle turned and walked up to the screeching alpaca that seemed to calm at her touch.

"Hey," she said into the phone.

"Hey, yourself. Any chance you have time to meet for coffee at Green Bean?" His deep timbre came across the line and soothed her rough edges. Maybe instead of coming to the alpaca farm, she should have called Raf. But then she wouldn't have had the chance to see Brielle again.

"Aren't you at work?" She checked the time on her phone. The workday was still in full force for those who had a job. Well, now she seemed to have a business. At least a business idea.

"Took the day to supervise my brother and father moving in."

"So, you said yes. Good for you." She was proud of him for taking a chance. She stole a glance at Brielle laughing with the alpaca. Hopefully, her sweet cousin would find it in herself to take a chance too.

"We'll see. I may regret it. Ember, do me favor, though."

"What's that?" Strip naked for him? That she would gladly do and might try tonight. She practically skipped back to the car. She was ready to go back to Raf's place. She would return to the alpaca farm another time and visit with Brooklyn later.

"Stay away from them while you're living with me."

"Why?" She stopped with her hand hovering above the door handle.

"Because I don't trust them."

"Raf, I think you're overreacting." His family problems had nothing to do with her. Johnny and Tino wouldn't even notice her being there. He was almost sounding like her father.

"Please just promise me."

"What if they try and talk to me? Am I supposed to ignore them?" She slid into the car and headed down the driveway.

"Just don't go into the house unless I'm home. And don't take rides from them. And don't let them in my house if I'm not there."

"I was on my way there now. Where am I supposed to go? And honestly, Raf, I don't want to live like a prisoner. Would it be better if I found somewhere else to hang until I find a place of my own? You're making them sound dangerous."

"They can be dangerous."

"Then why did you say yes?" She turned right without much of a destination for the second time today.

"Because you asked me to." He choked out a laugh.

"I highly doubt that I'm the reason you caved. You're a big softy, whether you want to admit it or not, and you're very good at taking care of others. Besides, I think you're overreacting when it comes to your family. It's going to be fine. You'll see."

"I'll try not to be paranoid where Johnny and Tino are concerned. But please be aware when you're around them."

"Yes, sir." She mock saluted even though he couldn't see her.

"Come on, I'm not trying to be an overprotective man who thinks his woman can't take care of herself."

"So, I'm your woman now?" She liked the sound of that.

"Only if you want to be. And you don't have to answer that. What do you say? Meet me for coffee."

"Well, since you told me I can't go back to my house unless you're there, I guess a coffee with a sexy Spanish man will have to do."

"Meet you there."

She ended the call and turned left toward town with a warm feeling in her chest. Things were looking up.

Then her phone rang.

CHAPTER TWENTY

Raf sent his third text to Ember. She hadn't answered his calls either, and she hadn't made it to the coffee shop where he was still waiting. The sun was starting to set and a light drizzle coated every surface. The rain would be good for the trees, but he wondered if the slick roads had sent Ember into a spin or worse.

He dumped his coffee in the trash and gave a wave to Jameson, who owned the garage across the street, sitting at a table by himself. Jameson held his cup up in a return gesture. Raf made a quick turn and stopped at the table.

"Hey, Jamie. How's it going?"

"All good. Heard your dad was back in town." Jamie leaned back in his chair and scratched at his jaw.

"For now. You didn't get any calls in the last hour for a tow, did you?"

"It's been quiet today. Something happen?"

"I don't know. Probably not. Thanks. I'll let you get back to your coffee."

"See you around then."

"Yeah. See you." He hurried to his truck. Ember will probably make fun of him for worrying about her and tell him he needed to stop because she could take care of herself. But she couldn't do that if her car had crashed into a tree.

His house was close. He would head there first. Maybe she had stopped to change and lost track of time. She didn't want to heed his warnings about Johnny and Tino. And maybe he was overreacting, but he had no reason to trust either of them completely. That would take some time.

He pulled into the driveway, but her little blue rental wasn't there. He sent another text just in case.

Tino came around the back of the house in a windbreaker with the hood up. He spotted the truck and trotted over. "What are you doing back so soon? You decided you wanted to help us unpack?"

He ignored Tino's attempt at humor. "Did you see Ember since I left?"

"So, she is living with you. How did you pull that off so fast? You weren't even dating two weeks ago and now she moved in. I've got to give it to you. You've got some mad skills when it comes to the ladies."

"Don't be disrespectful. Jesus. She's renting a room. I would have rented her the entire apartment next door if you hadn't trashed the hell out of it."

"Sorry." At least Tino had the decency to look remorseful.

"Did you see her or not?" Time was ticking. Each minute she was missing had him thinking the worst.

"Not me. Doesn't she have a couple of sisters? Anyone I could date?"

He wanted to get out of the truck and pop his brother. "Please shut up. If she comes back, and you see her, text me. Don't go up to her."

"Why not? Does she bite or something?" Tino howled at his own joke and slapped his leg.

"Because I don't want you talking to her."

Tino snapped to attention. "Is she too good for me? Is that what you're saying? Because then she's too good for you. We've got the same blood. I know where you came from. You can't pretend to be some big hotshot at the orchard. I know what a loser you really are."

"Don't start this now. I have to go." He put the truck in reverse.

"Now seems like a good time." Tino gripped the door. Anger raged across his eyes. His jaw was clenched.

"Let go, or I will run you over."

"You talk tough, Rafael. But I know you're not all that. You cave to all of us like we're homesick puppies needing their mamma. Ax begged you to take Johnny in and you said yes because you don't have a backbone. Even though Johnny is the reason all of our lives have been hard. He's the reason for all our problems. He made you give up college and life of your own. He's the reason you follow Brad Wilde around, always kissing his ass. Like you'd ever be as good as him. You're not in that league. You never will be. And you have Johnny to thank for that. But what do you do? You give him a place to stay."

He shoved the door open, knocking Tino back. He gripped Tino by the shirt collar and hoisted him until they were nose to nose. "Listen to me good because I won't say it again. Your screwups are your fault. You're a damn grown-up now. When are you going to stop blaming Daddy for your problems?" He pushed Tino away hard enough he stumbled.

The bravado left Tino's eyes. Deep down he would always be the little brother afraid of his father and cautious of Raf.

Tino tugged his shirt into place. "My life would've been better if both parents had died when I was born. They screwed everything up. Took every chance away from us. When are you going to see you won't amount to anything other than the second guy at the orchard? You think you're going to run the place someday? That's a laugh. You aren't their family."

"I thought you came back here actually sorry for what you did to my home and me. I've always tried to help you. But you don't see that. You're so mad at Johnny and Mom that you can't see beyond your own nose. Get over it, Santino. The world doesn't owe you a thing."

He hopped back in the truck and tore out of there before he did something stupid like punch Tino in the face or run over his foot just to make a point. He stole a glance in the rearview mirror. Johnny stood on the porch, shaking his head.

No matter what he had just said to Tino, he did blame Johnny Alvarez for making their lives harder than they had to be. The difference between him and Tino was he wasn't still angry about it.

∼

Ember closed the door to her parents' bedroom, then found her father in the kitchen staring out the window.

"She's asleep."

"If this rain keeps up, it won't be good for the apple trees. We'll be dealing with rot and disease," her father said as if she hadn't spoken.

She had no idea how much rain was good for the orchard or not. Her father would know every piece of planting information right down to the inch of rain required. He wasn't looking for a confirmation or an objection. He was making an observation as if this were any other day.

"Dad, we need to talk about Mom's care."

He held on to the sides of the sink and hung his head. "This is our problem. I will handle it."

"Let me help you. That's why I'm here."

"I didn't ask you to come here and help me. This is all Petra's fault. If the hospital hadn't called her first instead of me, none of you three girls would have known about the mishap in the store."

"We want to help you. You don't have to do this alone."

"You don't understand."

"Then please help me."

He turned to look at her. It was as if her father had aged a decade in an afternoon. His skin sagged around his jawline when it had been snug there before. His eyes were red and dark half-moons hung below them. "I can't help you. I'm helping your mother."

"You're right. I don't understand."

"Leave me be. You can come by tomorrow after I

leave for work." He turned away from her and stared out the window.

She hesitated, trying to find something to say to convince him to let her help. There had to be families all over the planet who wanted their children to get involved and share the burden. Here she was, offering her time and attention, and both of her parents continued to turn her away.

"You don't think I'm smart enough or reliable enough or enough of something to help. That's it, isn't it? Your three daughters are such a letdown."

"I have never said that." He stood his full height and roared like he used to when he was young and had come home from work wanting a quiet house and dinner on the table.

She flinched, but she couldn't stop. She wasn't a child anymore and would not be afraid of her father. "It's because I'm not a man. If you had sons, you would be enlisting their help, right?"

"You don't know what it's like to be a parent. My guess is you never will. Your mother wants to protect you and your sisters. And if she had sons, she would want to protect them too. Now go, Ember. I don't want to talk anymore." He turned back to the window again as if he could find answers in the rain.

He ran a hand over his face. His shoulders shuddered. She had never witnessed her father defeated and it sent a frozen chill down her spine. She reached out a hand but pulled it back as if she might get burned. Then did what he asked and turned to go.

CHAPTER TWENTY-ONE

F ire continued to burn in Raf's veins from his fight with Tino. He hoped no one crossed him because he would take that anger out on whoever was the fool. If Huck said one thing wrong about him or his family or his dating Ember, Raf would blow a gasket. He had enough of everybody's self-righteousness for one day.

He tore into the long driveway leading to Huck's house. The house was old and tired, a lot like Huck was. All that hatred inside Huck would kill him someday. Or it would pickle him to live forever. This wasn't the first time he wondered how it was Huck acted like he did when his brothers and his father were so different. Was the man dropped on his head as a baby?

The rain had picked up since he left the coffee shop. He hoped it didn't last much longer. The trees didn't need any extra rain right now. Just like he didn't need any extra trouble from Tino, but like the fungus that could grow in the soil, Tino was becoming a fungus that would cause nothing but sorrow. He felt it in his bones.

He didn't have to pull in all the way. Ember's car was parked near the house. Something terrible must have happened to Ruby. He jumped out of the truck and ran.

But he stopped short. Ember sat on the porch steps, pressed up against the banister and getting soaked by the rain. Her hair hung in wet clumps over her shoulders. Her clothes were soaked and clinging to her skin. She shivered where she sat.

"Ember? Are you okay? What happened?" He wrapped an arm around her to lift her to her feet.

She went willingly, which he was glad for. Because if he had to, he would throw her over his shoulder and put her in the truck. If Huck had done this to her, he would march inside that house and let that man have it once and for all. To hell with his job, his relationship with Brad. To hell with all of it, if Huck hurt Ember like this.

He led her to the truck, helped her inside, and ran around to slide in beside her. He blasted the heat, wishing he had a blanket or even a jacket to put on her.

"Ember, can you speak? Is it your mom?"

She held her hands up to the vents. "My father."

"I'll take care of it." He knew it. He would throttle Huck.

Ember grabbed his arm, stopping him from getting out of the truck. "It's not what you think. I saw my father crying."

"That's what had you sitting in the rain?" It would have shocked him too. "Do you want me to go inside and check on him?"

"God, no. Please don't do that. I think he's falling apart. I never saw him that way before."

"If you're sure, then let's get you back to the house

and dried off. You can tell me the whole story." He tapped the gas pedal a little harder.

"I don't know the whole story. They won't tell me. It's like they're hiding something, but I can't figure out what it is. Why don't my parents want me to help them?"

"Your father is a very independent man. He's used to being in charge and telling other people what to do. He probably wants to be the only one to decide how to handle your mother's condition."

"That's so selfish of him. He's denying me my chance to say goodbye to my mother."

"Maybe. Maybe not." Huck had always been a selfish man. At least as far as Raf could see. Huck made decisions where his family was concerned even when those decisions had nothing to do with him. Like when he had decided last fall to try to break up Caleb and Brooklyn.

"How did you know where I was?" She looked at him. The color in her face had not returned. The edges of her lips were blue.

"You never showed up at Green Bean. I got worried so I went looking."

"I'm sorry."

"You don't have to be sorry." He reached over and took her hand. Her skin was the temperature of a lake before the sun had risen high enough to warm the water.

"Raf, why do you want to be involved with me?" She pulled her hand away and sat on it.

"Let's talk about this later. You need to get warm and dry." He raced the yellow light and hoped a police officer wasn't anywhere around. He would have to do some fast talking if he got pulled over.

"I need to know."

"We're at the house. Let's talk when we get inside." He didn't wait for a response and jumped out. He wanted her behind closed doors before Tino or Johnny had a chance to stick their faces out the window and start asking questions.

He kept her close as he led her up the porch and into the house. "Go into the laundry room. I have clean sweats in there you can borrow. They're folded in the basket. Throw your clothes in the dryer. I'll make you some soup."

He would have gladly grabbed the clothes and placed hers in the dryer, but she would not want him to even suggest it. If she needed him, then she would have to say it.

"Thank you. I'll be right back."

He moved around the kitchen, opening a can of soup and dumping it in a pot. He had never mastered the art of cooking. He hadn't seen the point for just him, and it was mostly just him over the years. He hadn't bothered to let a woman get too close. Not until Ember showed up.

He wouldn't answer her question about why he wanted to be with her, because he would sound crazy if he tried to express how he felt. There had not been a getting to know you period where a person learns the other's attributes. He had taken one look at her at the train station, and his heart had stuttered. He had looked into those blue eyes and wanted to get lost in there. How was a woman who was so stubbornly independent and with Huck as a role model going to take to that answer? She would want a diagram with charts and pulse rates and blood pressure statistics. Until her, he had had no idea he could even be romantic. And now that was all he wanted to be around her.

"That smells good." She had returned in his sweatpants that she had rolled up at the ankles and a Wilde Orchards sweatshirt that swam on her. Her hair was still wet, but maybe a little less. The pink had returned to her lips. And she was the most beautiful woman he had ever seen.

"It's from a can." He grabbed a couple of ciabatta rolls from the drawer and tossed them in the air fryer.

"It's perfect. Thank you." She took a seat at the kitchen table and tucked her legs under her. "And thank you for coming for me. I don't know how long I sat out there."

"Can you tell me why you chose to sit on the porch in the rain and not in your car? I know what you said about Huck being upset, but there had to be more." He pulled down two bowls from the cabinet.

"The whole day had become too much. I had a fight with my mother this morning. She told me she didn't want me to help her. And if that was the reason I came to Candlewood Falls, I should go. What she said... it hurt so much. Why would she push me away like that? I swear my heart broke in two pieces."

"Your mom is going through something awful. She doesn't mean what she says." He brought the bowls to the table and took the seat opposite her. He had tried therapy once in his early twenties. He had learned that people with illnesses, mental and physical, often said things they didn't really mean. The illness made them act differently than they would have otherwise.

"I think she does mean all of it. She's so clearheaded

and calm when she says it. Look, I can't imagine what she's going through. I just want to make her feel better. I want to make myself feel better. You know, make up for the times I wasn't the best daughter. Is that wrong?"

"Not at all." The air fryer dinged. He popped the door open and juggled the hot bread back to the table. "But I have a feeling you weren't the bad daughter you think you were."

"I don't know. I'm sure I said terrible things to her when I was a kid." She pushed vegetables around in her bowl, pushing them under the soup and then letting them bounce back up.

"We all said things we shouldn't have. Especially as a teenager." He had and he had believed Johnny deserved to hear every one of them. Maybe he had. Or maybe Johnny had actually tried to do his best. His best sucked, but that didn't mean he hadn't tried.

"I suppose. I went for a ride after she and I fought and ended up at the alpaca farm. I bumped into my cousin Brielle who I haven't seen in ages. We caught up a little. It was nice. For a second I didn't think about being Huck's daughter while I was around a relative."

"I know that feeling."

"You do?" She continued to stir the soup, but she didn't take a bite.

"Sure. For years, I thought everyone would judge me by my parents. First my mother, the drug addict. Then Johnny who was a thief and a cheater and a liar. I thought people would pity us because what kind of a father walks out without a look back? Maybe it was somehow my fault that he left."

"Oh, Raf." She grabbed his hand. "His leaving wasn't your fault. You have to know that."

"I do now." It had taken years to figure it out. When he had, he could put some of the anger away, pack it up for good. "I just didn't want anyone thinking I was like him."

"You're not. You aren't anything like him."

"You don't know him."

"I know you well enough to know that you couldn't be. You have never once abandoned your brothers. You have been there for them every step of the way. You allowing Tino to come back and live next door is proof of that."

He didn't know what to say. His motivations for giving Tino another chance were unclear to him. Sure, he had made a promise to always help his brothers no matter what, but Tino had crossed the line when he stole from the orchard. He couldn't forget that. In fact, Tino would have to make amends with Brad and Silas. He would insist on it.

"I will say this." She tore a piece of the bread off and shoved it in her mouth. "If Johnny gave you anything, it was only his good parts."

"Johnny doesn't have any good parts." He kept his gaze on his food.

"Would you say the same about Huck?" She gripped his wrist, forcing him to look up.

"For all Huck's flaws, he made you. I'll have to thank him for that."

"Don't thank him too fast."

"So, what else happened today?" He decided butter would be good with the bread even if it was cooling down. He grabbed some of that too and a knife. Ember took the knife from his hand and buttered their rolls before he even sat back down.

"I was getting in the car to come and meet you." She put the bread down and looked at her lap. Her hair fell over her face.

He brushed it away so he could see her. She gave him the thinnest of smiles.

"My mother had called me. I didn't realize what was happening when I first answered. She was screaming. Calling my name over and over." She worked her bottom lip under her teeth.

"You don't have to talk about it if you don't want to."

She shook her head. "I thought maybe the house was on fire or maybe my dad had collapsed or something. But it wasn't that. I finally got her to focus enough to tell me what happened. She was frightened because she didn't know where my dad was. He wasn't home. That was all it was, but she had thought something terrible had happened and wanted to call the police."

"Your dad was at work." He knew a little about dementia and how sometimes the person with the disease would get upset if they couldn't find their caregiver.

"She had been so clear this morning. She had even pointed it out. Maybe our fight caused the onset? I don't know. Maybe it was going to happen anyway. I said I would be right over. On the ride there, Petra and Nyx called me. She had called them too, looking for my father."

"How does she remember your phone numbers?"

"We have a note by every phone that says in case of an emergency to dial us."

"Smart planning. I'm guessing your father came home and you two went at it as well."

"Something like that. But he was so upset at the end of our conversation. More upset than I have ever seen him. I didn't even know my father could cry. He didn't shed a single tear when my grandmother passed. All her other sons did. Huck didn't even cry when his brother SJ was murdered. Murdered. At SJ's funeral, he was stone-cold. You must have noticed that. Weren't you there too?"

"People deal with grief in all different ways." He had been at SJ's funeral, but he didn't remember Huck's reaction. He had been focused on Brad and Silas. Silas had been hit hard when SJ was found dead in an alley. To this day, no one knew what actually happened that night. SJ's death might always be one of Candlewood Falls' unsolved mysteries.

"Apparently they do. Today I saw my father break down. It had never occurred to me until I was sitting in the rain that he actually loves my mother. Deep down love. Her illness is killing him too. I think that realization is what brought me to my knees. I couldn't take another step."

"What do you want to do now?"

"That's the thing. I don't know. They both told me to go. That they don't want me to help. That they're sparing me and my sisters some kind of burden. I don't know what I'm doing here. I gave up my apartment. I quit my job. And now I can't help my mother. My life is a mess. And then I feel badly for even thinking that because she has it so much worse than I do."

He stood and pulled her against him. She wrapped

her arms around his waist and rested her head against his chest. She was warmer than she was a little while ago. He closed his eyes and breathed in the sweet smell of her hair.

"You don't need to decide right now what to do with your life." He would keep his home open to her for as long as she wanted. He could help her find a job. There must be something she could do at the orchard for the time being.

She eased back to look up at him. "I asked you earlier why you wanted to be involved with me. I need to know, Raf. Because I can't be here for the wrong reasons. And I'm afraid I am."

CHAPTER TWENTY-TWO

Her words were a punch to the throat. Raf backed away from the embrace, trying to suck in air. He stared at Ember. "Are you saying you regret what's happened between us?"

"No regrets. I really like you. But I have to fix my life, don't you think?"

"My life is a mess too, Ember. But you're the one good thing in it. Why would I want to give that up while I'm trying to work through things with my family?"

"I don't want to screw up what we have while I'm trying to find my way. And I will. I always do." She moved farther away as if she wanted to put the space between them.

"Where is this coming from?" The confident, independent woman was slipping away and revealing her underside—who Ember might have been long ago.

"I need some space. That's all. Can you give me some space?" She gathered the bowls still filled with the untouched soup and left them by the sink.

"What does that mean? Do you want to stop seeing each other or do you just want to move out?" How could what they have be over before it barely got started?

"Maybe both. Can I have a few hours to figure out where I'll go?"

"You can stay here. I'll go." He could crash somewhere else for a little while. She believed she had no support system in place. He was certain her cousins would take her in, but she wouldn't want their help. And truthfully, he didn't want her to go. If she stayed here, there would still be a connection for them.

"That's crazy. This is your home."

He couldn't be here without her. She was everywhere now. He would picture her sitting on the couch or at the kitchen table. Every time he went into his room, he would see her naked in his bed. He'd have to burn those clothes because he would forever imagine her in them.

"Stay here for as long as you need. I'll grab some clothes and move in next door."

Her mouth fell open and her eyes grew wide. "You don't have to do that."

"It will be fine. Like you said, it's my house. If I have to, I'll throw them out."

"Okay." She gave one big nod and blew a breath out. "Thank you. I'll work on finding a new place first thing in the morning. I just want to lie down for a little while now."

"I'll be out of your hair in ten minutes." He went into his room and grabbed a duffel bag. He threw clothes and a toothbrush in without much care.

The rain pounded the roof. He texted one of the men on his team to check on the trees. Then he dropped onto the bed. He could sleep in the office at the orchard, but then he would have to explain himself. Huck would have a good laugh at his expense, knowing he'd been dumped by Ember.

He could stay at Brad's, but he didn't have the stomach to watch him and Lyra in love. He didn't begrudge his best friend his happiness, but he didn't want a front row seat at the moment.

Anywhere else would be too public unless he left town. He didn't want to go far in case Ember changed her mind.

That left one place. He would, in fact, have to go next door and live with Johnny and Tino. God help him.

He grabbed his phone and sent a text to Tino.

Unlock the door. I'm coming over.

Ember bit back tears as Raf closed the door behind him. He hadn't said a word as he passed her in the hall. The pain had etched lines on his face and placed a sadness in his eyes.

She had just thrown the man out of his own home. What the hell was the matter with her? Okay, he had volunteered to go next door because she had nowhere else to go at the moment. Which was just like the chivalrous Rafael. The angel of healing. He was giving her the space she had requested, and it drove her mad. He was right. She couldn't have her cake and eat it too.

She either needed to stay and see where this relationship went, or she needed to leave Candlewood Falls for good.

Her body ached, and her head pounded. She did want to lie down and forget about the day. She wanted to forget the frantic cries of her mother over the phone. That memory may haunt her for days. She also wanted to forget that she saw her father cry. It made him too human.

Those tears softened him in a way she didn't understand. And maybe couldn't accept. If she did, it would change everything she believed to be true about him. How could she have been so wrong about him? There had always been another side tucked away. Her mother had been able to see it when no one else could.

She cleaned up the kitchen and wiped the counters because it gave her something to do to ease the guilt of sending Raf next door. He didn't want to live with his father or brother. And thanks to her pushing him, now he would.

She wanted to bake. Her car was still at her parents' house and the recipe book was still inside the car. Raf had a tablet in the living room. She ran to see if he had grabbed it. He hadn't. She would pull up a recipe and bake. Maybe that would be the thing to clear her mind and push the draining fatigue away.

She scoured his cabinets for ingredients and came up with enough stuff to make a flourless cookie. His cookie sheets were old and terrible. He didn't have any parchment paper. So she lined the sheets with foil and used nonstick spray. It was all she could manage in a pinch.

She worked the ingredients, repeatedly checking the recipe for the next step. She preferred to make cookies she was familiar with, but she wasn't about to ask Raf to go and get her book or the missing ingredients. And he would too.

As she spooned the dough onto the cookie sheets, her thoughts slowed and her senses stepped in. The scents of peanut butter and vanilla danced under her nose. When the last of the dough was on the sheet, she licked the spoon. The coarse salt prickled her tongue. These cookies would be good when they were done.

While the cookies baked, she searched online for information about starting her own business. And then an idea popped into her head like the oven timer going off. She grabbed her cell phone.

"Hey, Brad, it's Ember. Could I pick your brain?"

CHAPTER TWENTY-THREE

"Don't ask." Raf hurried through the front door. He wanted to get upstairs before anyone could start firing questions. He wasn't in the mood to explain himself. Maybe going to Brad's would have been a better idea. Here he would be trapped under their judgmental gazes. He had certainly judged his father and Tino a time or two.

"What happened? Lovers' fight?" Tino sat on the couch with the remote pointed at the television and a mirthless smile on his face. Johnny sat in a nearby chair with a book in his lap, holding up his hands in surrender.

"I said don't ask." He took the steps two at a time.

The smallest of the three bedrooms was filled with packing boxes in all different sizes. When had Tino collected so much stuff? Johnny must have brought some of this, but all of it? The boxes took up enough space to leave a small path to the window that exposed the dark-blue carpet he had never gotten around to pulling up.

He stepped back out into the hallway. His head pounded. "Come and move some of these boxes out of here and put them in the basement."

What was he doing? He gave Ember his house so he would have to live here with these two boneheads. As if life wasn't already hard enough, and he had just made it ten times harder. He would have to text her in the morning with a time frame. He would not, could not, stay here indefinitely.

The knocking of knuckles on wood interrupted his thoughts.

"What's up, Johnny?" The only piece of furniture in this room was a bed. His last tenant had been a couple of years ago. A guy going to school in Princeton who couldn't afford the rent there.

"I wanted to see if you were okay." Johnny shoved his hands in his pockets and leaned against the doorjamb.

"I'm fine." He had no other choice at the moment.

"You look like you might break someone in two. I recognize the scowl. I've seen it in the mirror a time or two."

"If you and Tino can get all this crap out of here in the next twenty minutes, everyone will stay in one piece. I can't even get to the bed." He grabbed a box with the word whittling knives scrawled on it in marker and shoved it at Johnny.

His father glanced at the word and put the box down. "You never told me. Do you still play with wood?"

"Sometimes. I guess that box was mine. You can leave it in the hallway."

Johnny moved it. "I still dabble a bit. Keeps the mind

quiet." He tapped his skull. "You want to sit out back sometime and carve a few pieces?"

"No, thanks." He actually wouldn't mind sitting out in his shed, drinking a beer, and making another chess piece. But not with Johnny. Those days were over.

"Let me know if you change your mind. Are you sure you don't want to talk about whatever's bothering you?"

"When did you become a talker? You used to swing first and ask questions later."

Johnny ran a hand over his face and scratched at his jaw. "You're right. I never thought about what I was doing back then. I'm sorry for that."

"You have a lot to be sorry for."

"I made one bad choice after another. I wish I could go back and change all that. But I can't. I can help you now, though, if you'll let me."

"I don't need your help. I have everything under control." He almost laughed at how stupid that sounded.

"Then why are you sleeping here for the night when your Ember is next door? Is it over between you two?" Johnny grabbed another box off the bed and put that one in the hallway too.

Over. It had barely started. He didn't even know what he was so upset about. She needed space. She could have all the space in the world once he went back to his side of the house.

"We were never a thing."

Johnny arched a brow. "That's not what it looked like to me."

"How would you know? You saw us together once."

"Did I ever tell you about when I met your mother?"

"Please don't."

Johnny grabbed another box off the bed and went into the hall. "Santino, get your backside up here now and help your brother. Earn your keep, son." Johnny turned back to him. "I walked into Britten Bar. It was a dive bar on the back end of town. It's not there anymore. The place was packed. I was with my crew. We were looking for some guys who had hustled us in a game of pool. But when I saw her... man, I couldn't see anything else. It was like I was blind except for her. I forgot all about why I was in the bar in the first place."

"That's great, Dad. Love at first sight. Was she high?"

Johnny faltered. "What did you say?"

"I asked if she was high the night you met her. In other words, did you know right away she had a drug problem and you knocked her up anyway?" Calling him Dad had slipped out by accident. It must have been the way Johnny's face softened as he remembered the night his parents met. For a millisecond, the father he had wanted, who had shown up in the smallest of ways, had appeared in his hallway. Forgetting wouldn't happen again.

"I loved your mother. She's the only woman I ever really loved. Because I had it so bad for her, I didn't know how to help her. I wanted to do anything to make her pain go away. So, I got her the drugs. I shouldn't have done that either. I should have gotten her help. If your lady needs help, Rafael, get it for her."

"She asked me to give her space." And by doing what she asked, wasn't that helping her? If the woman didn't want him, he wasn't about to beg. He grabbed another box and dumped it in the hall. "Where is Tino?"

Johnny stepped around him. "Santino, get up here now. Your brother can't sleep in this mess." Johnny pushed a box down the hall near the stairs. "That boy. When will he ever learn?"

"He's a man. I think the problem is we all forget that. Tino has to figure life out for himself. We can't do it for him. I'll take the boxes down myself." He hoisted one into his arms and went downstairs.

Johnny was fast on his heels with a box of his own. "Santino?"

No sound came from the living room. Not even the television. He dropped the box by the basement door and went to look. Johnny peered over his shoulder. His fruity aftershave made Raf's eyes water.

"Oh, Dios. You can't say nothing to him." Johnny grabbed a piece of paper Tino left on the table. "He wrote a note."

"Where did he go?" Raf took it.

Carry your own boxes. I have plans. Don't know when I'll be back. Don't wait up. T.

He crumpled the note in his fist and tossed it on the floor. "What plans did he have?"

"Beats me. We may be living in the same space, but he hasn't said two words to me the whole time. I asked him what time he wanted to start patching walls tomorrow and he just walked out of the room."

"Bringing him here was a mistake. I should never have let Ax talk me into it." He had foolishly believed Tino was actually sorry when he had said it. But nothing ever changed with Tino. He had handed over a fistful of cash and expected to be forgiven.

Johnny gripped his shoulder. "Give him time. He'll come around."

"And what if he doesn't? I'm not bailing him out again."

"He's just out for the night. Nothing is going to happen. You'll see."

Raf couldn't sleep. The room was too hot. The window didn't open. And all he could think about was Ember. He didn't want her to leave town, but he didn't know how to make her stay. Not that he could make her do anything. She had to want to stay. If he wasn't a good reason, then she should do what her heart told her to do. He couldn't help but wonder if Huck had been a kinder man, would she be in this predicament?

He threw his legs over the side of the bed and rubbed his face with his hands. She hadn't sent a text or called. He grabbed a pair of jeans and shoved in his legs. Johnny's door was closed, but the door to the room Tino was using—the matching one he used on his side, the biggest one—was open. He poked his head in. The bed was empty. Raf checked the time on his phone. Three in the morning. Where the hell could Tino be? What bushes was he throwing up in this time?

He walked in bare feet downstairs and flipped on the light in the kitchen. Dishes filled the sink and the room stunk of broccoli and soy sauce. His fingers ran over a mountain of sticky crumbs on the counter. The refrigerator was as empty as Tino's room except for the leftover take-out containers from the dinner stinking up his kitchen and a half-full carton of eggs and a drop of milk in the plastic jug.

He could slip in next door without Ember noticing and grab a snack, then come right back. "Don't be an ass," he said to himself.

If he couldn't eat and couldn't sleep, there was only one place else he could go at this hour. He grabbed his keys, but before he went out back, he checked to make sure Tino wasn't passed out on the couch or the front porch. Both places were clear.

He went out the back slider and crossed the wet grass. The blades squished between his bare toes and soaked his feet. He quickly glanced over his shoulder. Ember's side of the house was dark. The window was open in his bedroom. Well, at least she would get a good night's sleep.

He unlocked the shed and slipped inside, closing the door and turning on the lights. He had an old radio that caught the local New Jersey stations pretty well. He picked one with soft music to keep him company.

He selected the chess piece he had been working on a few weeks ago before his life turned upside down—the queen. An hour of shaping wood should clear his head enough for sleep. He still had to go to work, and he would need at least an hour or two. He sure didn't need to give Huck any other reasons to try and run him off the orchard.

Raf pulled out his stool, adjusted his light, and wrapped his thumb in duct tape to keep from cutting it while he carved. There had maybe been about ten years where Huck didn't try to get him fired. It was right after SJ died. He might not have cried at the funeral, but losing his oldest brother seemed to have taken some of the hate out of his sails. Grief had made Huck too tired to start fights. Huck mostly ignored him back then. He missed those years.

Sometime after that, Huck joined a group of men who had decided it was up to them to keep the streets of Candlewood Falls free from those they didn't like. The group was the Brotherhood of Watchmen. Huck had risen to the position of president. That's when the hate came back and the return of his mission to get him fired. Huck had never figured out Brad and Silas wanted him there.

The wood shavings coated the table and the floor. Did he still want to be at the orchard? The question knocked him sideways. Where else would he go? What would he do? He was good at his job and valued by the people he worked with. He was respected by the men under him and by his bosses who weren't bosses at all.

He stared at his dust-covered hands. Ember had wondered why he didn't sell the pieces that he had spent hours creating. The answer floated around just out of reach. He didn't like what he was thinking.

The shed was as warm as his room. Or maybe it was just him fighting off the thoughts of the past and working up a sweat doing it. He opened the door to let the cool breeze come through and wash over him. He would sleep out here for the rest of tonight. If sleep came at all because his mind hadn't stilled. Instead, it raced toward a belief he thought he had put to rest. But it hadn't taken more than his father's return to prove that belief had never gone away.

He tore off the tape, wiped his hands on a towel, and

grabbed the sleeping bag from the camping equipment he kept stored in the corner. He would clean up in the morning.

"Raf?"

He jumped and dropped the sleeping bag. "Ember. What are you doing out here?"

Ember stood in the doorway, the light from the shed turning her into a silhouette. The breeze lifted her hair off her shoulders and fluttered the hem of the t-shirt around her thighs. His t-shirt. He swallowed the hard knot in his throat.

"I can't sleep. I looked out the window and saw you standing in the doorway with the light on. I thought... I didn't think. I just came outside. I hope it's okay. I can go if you want."

He grabbed her hand and tugged her closer. She smelled like vanilla and peanut butter. "Were you baking?

"How did you know that?"

"Good guess." His heart swelled. "I'm glad you came outside. I know you said you wanted space, but I'm not sure I can let you go so easily." He was going to ruin everything by pushing her, but he couldn't stop himself.

"Raf..." She ran her fingers over his brow.

"Please, Ember. Let me be the person who helps you. Not the person you walk away from."

"Things are so complicated." She linked her fingers through his.

"I know. But they won't always be. And your father will have to get used to the idea of us. He doesn't have the right to tell us what to do." For a second, he had almost given in to the old beliefs that he wasn't good enough, but now that she stood before him, her presence here gave him the courage to hope she'd stay.

"He may not have the right, but he will try."

"I don't care."

"I guess I have less to worry about where we're concerned, if he's telling me to mind my own business regarding my mother. I just wish I knew why." She rested her head against his chest.

"I'll help you find that out. I promise. But promise me you won't leave." He ran his hand up and down her back. He wanted to get lost in her.

"I'm scared, Raf."

"If it helps, so am I. I've never felt this way about someone before. You swooped in and changed everything in a blink of an eye. I didn't even know that was possible."

"I had sworn I'd never date a man who worked at an orchard. I didn't want anyone who could be like my father. But here you are, nothing like him except for the address of your employment. You are my angel of healing."

"Huh?"

"Your name. Raphael was the angel of healing. You have healed my heart."

He didn't want to talk any longer. There was more to say, but it could wait. He tilted up her chin and kissed her.

She sighed against him, and his head spun. Her fingers tangled in his hair as she pulled him closer. The kiss deepened, along with his desire for more of her. He may never be able to get enough.

Their tongues played and chased. Her hands were on

his chest, setting him on fire. Every inch of him responded to her touch. He was under her spell, and he never wanted it to be broken.

Tonight would be the night that he fell in love. He only wanted to kiss and touch and protect her. He wanted to walk beside her and support her, this woman he had no business wanting, but couldn't stop any more than he could stop breathing.

He eased out of the kiss. "Let's go inside."

"I don't want to wait. Let's do it out here." She looked up at him through her lashes, her bottom lip set under her teeth.

"You want to make love in my shed?"

"I want to make love with you anywhere. Here. Out in the grass under the stars. In the back of your truck. I don't care where we are as long as we're together."

"The floor is hard. Wouldn't you rather be in a bed?"

"I know you'll make sure I'm comfortable." She wrapped her arms around his neck and kissed him again.

He would spend all his days making her life easier if she would allow him to, but he wouldn't say it now. Now was too soon and too fragile. They were like a budding tree in spring, waiting for the fruit to show. It was too easy to lose that fruit to the elements.

He laid the sleeping bag on the cleanest part of the floor. He closed the door and locked it from the inside. They didn't need any uninvited appearances and since he still didn't know where Tino was, he wasn't taking any chances.

She lifted the t-shirt over her head, revealing all of her beautiful body for him. She had nothing on under that shirt and suddenly his jeans were uncomfortable.

She leaned back on the sleeping bag and beckoned him with one finger and a sly smile.

Oh, yeah. He was hooked. He positioned himself between her legs, using his arms to support himself. He wanted to taste all of her and took a nip of her breast.

She lifted his chin. "On your back, mister."

"Yes, ma'am." He flipped them so she was on top of him and his hands held her backside. "Did you mean like this?"

"Not exactly." She straightened. "First we need to get rid of these." She expertly undid the button on his jeans and slid them over his hips. His erection through his boxer-briefs gave away exactly what she was doing to him.

"Very nice," she said.

"Just nice?" He pushed up on his elbows.

"Better than nice." She shoved him back down. "Incredible."

"I can live with incredible." He tucked his hands behind his head. "Go ahead. You can have your way with me now."

She choked out a laugh. Her lips and tongue left a trail from his collarbone to his navel and back up. Her hands ran over his skin as if she were trying to memorize him. He wanted to touch her too and lifted her up to him.

"Why did you stop me?"

"Because I don't want to be the only one using their hands."

"You aren't used to anyone taking care of you. You always want to be the giver. Let me please you tonight."

He cupped her face. Their gazes met. "You are

already giving me plenty of pleasure. More than you know."

"Let me show you what you mean to me."

"Just being with me like this shows me that, babe." He kissed her again.

This time together they explored all the places on their bodies that made their hearts race. Sweat ran down his back. The shed was too hot again, but this time for the very right reason. In all the touching, they had switched places and she was under him.

Her legs wrapped around his waist, making room for him. He entered her and soared to the stars at the same time. They rocked together in sync as if they'd rehearsed more often than not. She was a part of him he didn't even know he was without.

"More." Her hands gripped his ass and pulled him closer to her.

He did as the lady asked and gave her enough to have her calling out his name. He waited until he was sure her shuddering had stopped and then allowed himself to let go and follow her over the side.

He wrapped her in his arms and held her close as their breathing slowed down.

"Nice," she said.

"Just nice?" He eased back to get a good look at her.

She gifted him a high-powered smile. "Better than nice. Incredible."

"I can live with incredible."

CHAPTER TWENTY-FOUR

Ember's phone rattled against the kitchen counter. She handed a mug of coffee to Raf. "It's my father."

"You'd better get it, then. I'm going to take a quick shower." He kissed her forehead and sauntered off with a mischievous smile on his face.

A heat crept up her neck at some of the memories of the night before in his shed. They had made love twice before they dozed off. He had been right about the hard floor which she had second-guessed when she woke up with a pain in her hip.

On a deep breath, she swiped to answer the call. "Hi, Dad." She put the call on speaker.

"Hello, Ember. Did I... did I wake you?"

If her father only knew what had woken her up this morning. "I'm having my first cup of coffee. Is everything okay?"

"You left your car here yesterday and the keys inside it. How many times have I told you that's dangerous?"

"It's Candlewood Falls, and I was in your driveway. Who would steal a car from your driveway?" No one in the town would be dumb enough to try and steal from Huck Wilde. He'd chase them off his property with his hunting rifle.

"Never mind that. Thieves don't care. Always lock the door."

"Okay, Dad. I'll come get the car this morning, if that's what you're worried about."

"How are you getting here?"

She needed to deal with her father's disapproval of her relationship because it would never go away if she didn't. "Raf will drive me on his way to work."

"You shouldn't live there. It doesn't look good. And his father is back. I know Johnny Alvarez is renting the other house. He's bad news."

"I've got it handled. If the only reason you called was to warn me away from the Alvarez family, you can stop. I like Raf. A lot." She paused to let what she said sink in.

"You're making a mistake with that man. But that's not why I called. When you come and get your car, don't bother your mother today. She isn't herself still."

"She didn't bounce back from yesterday?" Her stomach hollowed out. This was happening too fast. She wasn't ready.

"Not yet. I'm sure she will. She always does." He sounded more confident than she felt.

"What do her doctors say about this?"

"I don't have time to get into details right now. I have to get to work too. Just leave her be today. I don't want you two to have another fight."

"Why can't you take the day off today? I'm sure Uncle Silas and Brad will understand." She wanted to tell him to be the kind of man her mother deserved. The kind of man Raf was. Raf would never leave her alone to deal with something horrible. He took care of the people he loved.

"Silas doesn't know everything I do. By the time I explain it all to him, I could have done it myself."

"Someone should stay with Mom. If you won't be there, then let me."

"For once, do as I ask. Why is that so hard for you girls? I'll be back right after lunch. She'll be fine."

"You two are the most stubborn people I have ever met. None of this makes sense to me. Do you hate me? Is that it? You don't want me there because you hate me. Admit it." Her voice shook. She took a deep breath to keep it under control.

Her father let out a long sigh. "I don't hate you. Your mother doesn't hate you. It's just what we want."

"But why? Can you tell me why?"

"Your mother wants to leave this world with her dignity. She wants you to remember her as the person she was. Not the person she'll become with this illness. It might take years; she might be able to slow it down, but it's coming. She doesn't want help, not with the daily things anyway."

"Then with what?"

"I've said enough. Leave your mother be today." He ended the call.

She slammed the phone down on the counter harder than she meant and cracked the screen.

"Hey, what's going on?" Raf came around the corner

with his hair still wet, his face freshly shaven, and wearing a blue work shirt and jeans.

She went to him and folded into his arms. "I just want to shut the rest of the world out."

"Breaking your phone is one way to go." He held her close and rubbed her back with his sure and steady hand.

In spite of the anger boiling her insides, she laughed. "My father…" She didn't have the energy to finish.

"What did Huck say now?"

"He said a whole lot of nothing. And I still don't understand why I can't visit with my mother when she isn't well."

He eased out of the embrace. "I know you don't like this, but maybe you should consider her wishes. Give her the space she wants."

"Like I had asked you to give me space."

"I didn't like it, Ember. It was eating me alive. I'm glad it didn't last long, but it was what you asked me for. I had to give it to you."

"I could barely go a few hours without you." She had regretted her decision to have him leave the second the door had closed. It wasn't until after she had baked seven dozen cookies that she knew she wanted to be with him. He was the one thing that made sense when he shouldn't.

"It's my charming personality." He tugged at his shirt collar and beamed.

She tossed a dish towel at him. He grabbed it midair and barked out a long laugh. "What are you going to do today?"

"I'm going to take the first steps toward my new business."

"When did that come about?"

"Last night. I want to be a baker. I know it's crazy, but since I've been here, baking has helped me stay sane. I'm calm when I do it, and honestly, I want to do it more. It's weird, right? Going from IT to baking. What do I know about baking anyway? Have you seen some of those baking shows? Those people are so talented."

He cleared the space between them and took her hands. "You will be an amazing baker. I've tested the product. You could probably sell them at the orchard. I'm sure Brad would give you space in the store."

"Do you think?" That idea hadn't occurred to her when she spoke with Brad. He had given her pointers on how to get started, the legal stuff. But that was it.

"You're a Wilde. Your family always sticks together."

"Not my part of the family." She brushed the painful thoughts away. "Never mind. I'm going to work on my business plan and do some baking, if you don't mind me messing up your kitchen."

"Mess up any room you'd like. The kitchen. The bedroom. Wherever."

"I'll save the bedroom for when you're back."

"I'll be home by four." He kissed her and headed out.

Raf smiled to himself as he closed the front door behind him. He couldn't believe his good luck. He had Ember back. Together they would figure out how to deal with their families.

He wanted to stop at the other apartment before he headed into the orchard. He knocked, but no one answered. He tried again before unlocking the door with his key.

"Hey, anyone up?" He shouted throughout the house. He didn't care that it was early and he was probably waking them up. Or maybe Johnny had left for work already.

"Good morning." Johnny came out of the kitchen with a metal lunch box and tall travel mug in his hand. "Did you want breakfast?"

"You make breakfast now?"

Johnny shook his head. "I can cook. I made two eggs. There's three more you can scramble up. There's also some bread for toast. Other than that, you're out of luck. I'm going to stop at the store on my way home from work and do a food shop. What can I get for you?"

Raf had to blink a few times to make sure he really was standing in the house he owned. His father was dressed and bright-eyed before eight in the morning. He had packed a lunch and made breakfast. Miracles would never cease.

"Um… I'm going to be staying at my place. Looks like I don't need to crash here after all."

"Good for you, hijo. She's a beautiful woman, and she makes you smile like I've never seen."

"How would you know how I smile, Johnny?"

"I've never seen any man smile like you are right now. I've got to go. I don't want to be late." Johnny patted him on the shoulder.

"Did Tino come back?"

"Sadly, no. He's not answering his phone either. I called Axel this morning. He hasn't heard from him. He'll show up."

"I don't like it. Something's wrong." The tightness in his chest made him believe it was true.

"You worry too much. Santino has learned his lesson. He probably stayed at a friend's house. He'll be back."

"I thought you were going to take him to work with you?"

"Not today, it seems." Johnny shrugged and turned for the door. He hesitated and turned around. "Can I meet your lady friend?"

"You met her."

"I mean I'd like to get to know the woman who is making my son so happy. Would that be okay?"

He wasn't sure if he wanted Ember and Johnny spending time together. He wasn't ready to trust his father. Johnny was putting on a pretty good act, but anything could change in an instant. He needed a track record of no disappointments before he risked Ember in his company.

"I'll think about it."

"I can live with that. Have a good day, Rafael." Johnny went through the door without another word.

He stood there a few more minutes as if he couldn't move. His father seemed to be a new person. He didn't know if he should trust that or not. Time would tell. It always did. And while he was busy trying to decide if Johnny was worth the time, he hoped Tino would come back in one piece.

CHAPTER TWENTY-FIVE

Ember needed her car. She had started mixing the ingredients for her mother's chocolate chip cookies. She knew the recipe by heart because she'd been baking it on her own for years. It was the staple item she brought to any friend's house.

The recipe called for shortening, which was not the healthiest of choices, though some shortenings were made without the trans fat now. But shortening sure did make the most scrumptious of cookies. She could substitute with butter, which Raf did not have enough of, or she could use coconut oil or vegetable oil. Also not in Raf's pantry. She'd have to talk to him about the vegetable oil. That could be used for a bunch of things besides baking.

After her phone call with her father, she hadn't wanted Raf to drive her over to her parents' house. She figured she'd be ready to face them after he returned home and she had baked several dozen cookies. The baking would relax her and help her decide which cookies to include in her business plan.

She could walk into town, but that would take an hour there and an hour back. She shot Brooklyn a text to see if she might be around.

Brooklyn responded with speed. *Sorry. Out of town with Caleb.*

Maybe Raf could take a break for a little while and at least come get her and take her to her car. She sent him a text too.

Any chance you have free time? Need my car.

Can't leave. Problem at work. Will be home late.

Walking it was. She grabbed her wallet, the key to Raf's house, and headed out. She could use the exercise and the fresh air would do her good and give her time to think.

"Well, if it isn't my big brother's new girlfriend." Tino tossed his car keys in his hand.

His hair was messed as if he might've just woken up even though it was almost noon. His clothes had that bent and creased look, suggesting he still wore yesterday's outfit. Raf had warned her away from Tino. She had thought he was overreacting.

"Hello, Tino. Rough night?"

He scratched his head and laughed. When he smiled, he looked a lot like Raf. Her heart softened a little. Tino had suffered at the hands of their father just as much as Raf had. Stealing was wrong, but maybe Tino wanted attention and didn't know any other way to achieve it, which was sad for a man his age, but not impossible to believe of him. He didn't appear to be destitute, which might excuse someone stealing food. If he were without a penny, Raf would always help him out. All Tino would have to do is ask his brother for the help. Families were so complicated and yet the very thing society taught them to rely on.

"You could say it was somewhat of a rough night. Was Raf looking for me?"

"I don't know." She knew the answer, but wouldn't give Raf away. He could discuss with Tino whether or not he had been worried about his brother's whereabouts. "If you'll excuse me, I'm headed into town for some groceries."

Tino searched the area. "Without a car?"

"I don't mind walking." The sun had broken free of the clouds. The air was cool, but she had borrowed Raf's heavy sweatshirt. She'd be fine on a walk unless the rain returned unexpectedly.

"It will take you forever to get to the heart of town. I can give you a ride. I was just going to grab something to eat and a nap anyway. I can do that later."

"No, thank you. I don't want to put you out."

"Hey, it's the least I can do for Raf's girlfriend. He would want me to make sure you got where you're going."

She was certain Raf would prefer she not walk on the windy, narrow country roads into town because he believed any fool could come around the corner too fast and knock her over. He wouldn't want her riding with Tino either. But they would only be in the car a few minutes. In fact, it would be closer to drive her to her own car. Then he wouldn't have to wait for her to do her shopping and bring her back. Raf wouldn't mind a quick ride. What could it hurt?

"Okay, thank you. But instead of town, can you drive me to my parents' place? My car is there."

"Sure thing." He tossed the keys again and swiped them out of the air with a wink. "I'd be happy to."

"It's the second driveway on the left." She pointed on instinct as Tino hit his blinker. He pulled into the driveway and parked behind her car.

"Nice house." Tino hopped out.

"Where are you going?" She hurried after him.

She didn't understand what he was doing. She hoped he wasn't expecting to be brought inside. Her mother would not want a stranger stopping by, and she would do what Raf suggested and give her mother some space.

Tino went closer to the house, inspecting it like a piece of art. "It's funny how you can live in one town your whole life and not know everyone."

"I'm not following."

"I'm just saying, I never knew Huck lived in such a big place. It must be worth a fortune." Tino scratched at his neck.

"It isn't that big." It was a moderate home with four bedrooms and the respectable number of baths. The formal living room was the largest room in the house, and a waste of space as far as she was concerned. The porch was always her favorite spot when she was a kid.

Tino turned to her. "When you grow up in a trailer with three brothers, this is a palace."

"I see." She was being a little paranoid. Tino was just making an observation of the differences in their upbringings.

"Can I have a tour?"

"What? Oh, no... no. I'm sorry. My mother isn't

feeling well. In fact, my father told me this morning not to disturb her when I came to get the car." Okay, not totally off-base. He had wanted to see inside, but she would not allow it.

Her father would have a coronary if he ever found out Tino was inside his home. He was still angry about Tino not getting sent to prison for robbing the orchard. They hadn't discussed it at length, but her father held a long grudge whenever he was wronged.

"What's wrong with your mom?"

She could simply say she had a spring cold or the flu, but she had to start accepting that her mom's illness would only get worse. They couldn't hide from it, even if it felt like that's what her parents were doing.

"She has early onset dementia." The words tasted like dust in her mouth.

"That's like forgetting things, right?"

"Pretty much."

"Does she know you?"

"Mostly. But sometimes she forgets that my sisters and I are grown. Or she forgets how to come home when she goes out. Sometimes she even forgets she's home alone."

"Yeah, Huck works a lot. So she's here by herself during the day?"

"She is unless I come for a visit which I do most days since I've been in town." She didn't want him thinking she was neglecting her mother by not staying all day while her father was at work. She would be doing exactly that if her parents would let her and every visit didn't end in a fight.

"That's nice of you." He offered her that warm smile that was so much like Raf's.

"Thanks for the ride, Tino." She opened her car door to give him the hint the conversation was over. She didn't want to linger any longer in case her mother peered out the window and saw them standing there.

Tino continued to take the place in. "How many windows does the house have? Looks like about forty."

"I've never counted." Such a strange question. Although she had seen a documentary once on homes with a more than the average number of windows. Every house had been bigger than this one, so maybe it wasn't such a strange question after all.

Growing up, she took her home for granted. It wasn't fancy, but it was certainly nicer than the cabin Uncle Silas, Brooklyn, and Brad lived in. Though Brooklyn and Brad never complained all that much. Ember always assumed it was because of how much they loved their father. If she had to live in a two-room cabin with her father, she might have gone stark raving mad.

Tino shrugged and returned to his car. "I hope your mom feels better." He slid into the car and drove away.

She stood there until the humming of the engine and the tightness in her belly were gone.

Raf let himself into the house. The smell of warm butter, sugar, and chocolate greeted him at the door like a new puppy. Ember must still be baking. Cookies for dinner would be exactly what he needed because he was too tired to cook anything for himself. His back and shoulders hurt from lifting and digging and carrying. He had spent the entire day putting out one fire after another. All so Huck could knock into him in the hallway as if he didn't see him.

"Seriously, Huck?" he had said.

"Didn't see you, Alvarez. Don't get your panties in a knot." Huck had laughed at his worn-out joke.

"How could you miss me?" He wasn't as tall or as broad as Brad, but for Christ's sake, he wasn't invisible.

"Just watch where you're going. That's all I'm saying." Huck pushed through the doors that led to the store area.

"What's that supposed to mean, Huck?" He had yelled after him, but like he had suspected, Huck ignored him. Brad had come out of his office to ask what all the yelling was about, but he had waved Brad away. He could handle Huck himself.

Now, he slid up behind Ember, standing at his sink. She wore a pink cotton dress that looked more like a t-shirt and barely hit the middle of her thighs. She had great legs. He wrapped his arms around her waist, pulling her against him. "I have wanted to do this all day."

She snuggled her butt against him, instantly turning him on. Maybe he wasn't so tired.

"I wanted you to come up behind me and press into me all day too." She put down the cookie sheet she was drying and swished her bottom across his hips again.

"Jesus, Ember." He nipped at her neck.

She leaned back into him, lifting her chin to increase his access to her neck. As he kissed and sucked her soft skin, she continued to sway against him until they were grinding.

"I'm losing my mind right now," he said against her hair.

"Let me help you with that."

Telling Raf she had been thinking about him coming up behind her was the truth. She hadn't been able to get the idea out of her head. When the door opened, and he had returned from work, she nearly came on the spot. She didn't know what was happening to her. Well, maybe she did.

She kept her back to him, then took his hands and led him over to the table.

"Can I ask what's happening right now?" The timbre of his voice dropped lower. The vibration of his words excited her more.

"Shh." She leaned against him again, placing one hand over her breast and the other around her waist.

"I think I see." He returned to kissing her neck. The tender touch of his lips sent shivers over her skin.

She pushed her behind harder into him and the ache between her legs grew stronger. "How was your day?"

"It's better now." His fingers kneaded her nipple through her dress until it became a hard knot. She wasn't sure if she could keep standing, but she wanted to go through with the plan that had planted itself in her mind.

She had purposely worn this dress. Easy access for him. Comfortable for her. "You had a bad day, then?"

"Let's talk about that later." His other hand slid lower

over her abdomen, but she stopped him before he could go any further.

"Not yet. Would you undo your pants for me?" She wasn't ready to turn around. She would after, when they were done. The jingle of his belt and the release of his zipper made her insides tingle. "Now slide your pants down. Underwear too."

The whoosh of denim over his legs buckled her knees.

"What are you going to do for me?" He spoke in a raspy whisper. Her plan was working.

Her heart pounded against her ribs as if it were an entire marching band. The craving between her legs consumed her. She had never trusted a man more. He had been a surprise and exactly what she needed when she hadn't known at all that she had.

She shimmied the dress above her waist, revealing that she had nothing on underneath. He sucked in a breath. She had been imagining this scenario with every cookie she had baked. Until the waiting nearly killed her. When he touched her, she would incinerate.

She draped herself across the table, giving herself to him.

"Dios mio," he said as he took her.

CHAPTER TWENTY-SIX

"Thanks, Brooklyn. I'll bring some by later today." Ember put her phone down and beamed at him. "She said she would take some cookies. I can't believe this is really happening."

Raf took in the sight of her standing at his kitchen counter. She radiated as if the sun had burst through her. Her hair was still mussed from sleeping. She wore his sweatpants again because the morning had been chilly, and no matter how many times he asked her to stay naked, she only laughed and said she had a million things to do and she couldn't very well do them with her bottom hanging out. He begged to differ.

"That's fantastic." He pulled her against him, needing her next to him. "Your first customer."

She pushed out of his arms and wiped her hair from her face. "Okay, I may be doing this backward. I probably need to incorporate or something first. I don't even have a logo or a company name." She spun in a circle. "I can't believe I'm actually doing this. Yes, I know I'm rushing—again. But I feel like I'm soaring. Does that make sense?"

"Before you showed up in my life, I might have said no. But you turned my world around like a much-needed wind on a hot day. So, yes. You make perfect sense to me."

"And I have you to thank for it."

"Me? I didn't do anything." He put his mug in the sink. He needed to get to work. He had sent a text to Brad saying he'd be a little late this morning. After the problems yesterday, he wanted an extra hour away from the orchard. He had also wanted more time with Ember.

She had blown his mind last night with that incredibly sexy show. If he continued to think about her sprawled over that table, he might never get to work. He might also need to bronze that table.

"Raf, did you hear me?"

"Sorry. Thinking about work." And her backside.

She returned to him and wrapped her arms around his neck. "I'm sorry. I'm going on and on about this new business and I never even asked what had happened yesterday at work."

He couldn't tell her it had involved her father and because of Huck there had been a huge screwup. He suspected Huck was off his game because of Ruby and didn't want to add to the problem she was having with her parents.

"It's done now. It doesn't matter. I have something to run by you, though."

"Sounds important. Let me give you my full attention." She leaned against the counter and crossed her arms over her chest. She arranged her face into a serious grimace.

He couldn't believe he was about to say this. "My father asked if he could get to know you better. What do you think?"

"That's it? I thought you were going to tell me you were ready to quit the orchard and start your own business too."

"I'll leave that to you. I'm fine where I am." And he was—most of the time. But lately, since Tino's return and demise, the orchard had lost some of its magic. He figured it was a phase, and he'd get back to his usual self. Probably in the fall when the apples needed picking. That was the busiest time at work.

"I still think you should consider doing something with your pieces."

"Maybe someday. I'm not sure if I'm ready to trust Johnny, but what do you think about spending time with him?"

"I think that would be nice." She shrugged as if that were the simplest of answers.

"I had a feeling you'd say that." He gathered his wallet and keys. He could take a page out of her book for one night. One night with Johnny couldn't hurt too much.

"If you don't try, you never will. We could have dinner together, the three of us. And even Tino if you want. Oh." She punctuated the air with a finger. "He gave me a ride to my car yesterday. I thought that was nice of him."

"Tino? You saw him? And you didn't tell me?"

"I forgot. When you came home I had other things on my mind." She wagged her eyebrows at him.

"He had been gone the entire night before." Granted, last night he had his mind on more important things than his brother, but Tino had no right to take off and not let anyone know where he was going. He could end up dead on the side of the road and no one would know. It was just like Tino not to consider anyone else.

"He's a grown man. He can do what he wants. You need to start letting him."

"You don't understand. He always finds trouble that he can't handle." She had not been there through the years. He had been the one to get Tino away from the guys selling drugs on the street. He had been the one to convince Tino to stay in school and graduate. He had been the one to make sure Tino got to his job because most of the time Tino didn't feel like going.

"You can't save him, Raf. Trying won't change anything."

"What does that mean?" If he stopped trying to help Tino, his brother would fail. Someone had to be in his corner.

"It means, no matter how Tino lives his life, your past is still your past. You can't fix what's already happened."

"I can sure as hell try to make up for it." He owed Tino that much. When he became his brothers' guardian, he had promised himself he would be the man Johnny had never been. He cooked and cleaned the trailer. He had found a job and went to work, giving each of them money when they needed it. He had attended conferences at school and sat through elementary school concerts for Tino. He had taken his brothers to the clinic when they were sick.

"Making amends for the past is not your job. That's your father's job, which it appears he wants to do, but you won't let him do that either."

"I'm not having this conversation now. I have to get to work." He dug his keys into his fist. She didn't understand. Even though Huck was a disagreeable human, he stayed put. He showed up every day for his family even if his only contribution was a paycheck. That money kept that big roof over their heads and their bellies full. Huck gave them an extended family by birth. Ember had a right to everything at that orchard. When Huck passed, his fifth of the orchard would go to his children.

When he died, his family — should he ever have one — would get nothing but the retirement plan he had been saving.

"Don't run away. Please, Raf. I don't want you to go to work mad."

"I'm not the one running." He marched out the door and slammed it shut.

She followed him outside. "I'm not running from anything. I'm staying put in this town and starting a business. Don't you dare accuse me of not dealing with my issues."

He stopped and turned. "Let me ask you something. Have you told your father our living arrangement has progressed and we're sleeping together?"

Her hesitation was all the answer he needed.

"That's what I thought." He jumped in the truck and kicked up dust as he drove away, leaving her on the porch.

"Lovers' spat?"

She jumped at the unexpected intrusion and found Tino leaning on the front door of his place with a smirk across his face.

"Where did you come from?"

"I could hear the fight. Thin walls. I came outside to make sure Raf didn't cross any lines." He kicked the porch with the toe of his shoe.

"Do you know your brother at all? What would ever give you the idea that he would hurt anyone?" She did not understand this young man, and she tried to remember what it was like to be his age. Back then, she had still believed all things were possible. Tino seemed to think nothing worked out for him.

"I know you're too good for him."

"Are you jealous of him? Is that why you're always at odds?" Never mind that she and Raf had another argument. Tino didn't realize how wonderful Raf was to him and how lucky he was to have Raf loving him.

Tino choked out a laugh. "Jealous of Raf? He doesn't have anything I want. Except for maybe you."

Her stomach turned sour. "Get a grip." She hurried inside and locked the door. She had enough of Alvarez men for one day. First Raf and his stubbornness to fix everyone and now Tino and his ungratefulness.

She gathered the ingredients and tools she had purchased yesterday and stuck them in a shipping box Raf had in the basement. She threw her clothes into her suitcase. If Raf was going to be a pigheaded ass accusing her of hiding from her father as if she were a high schooler afraid to get grounded, then she had better find another place to live.

Raf didn't know her at all. She pulled the suitcase zipper shut and snagged her finger. The pain shot up her hand.

She shoved her finger in her mouth to staunch the bleeding. "Damn it, Raf."

He was right. She had avoided telling her father the whole story. At first it was because she needed him on her side when it came to her mother's care. But her parents had effectively banned her from that task.

She had accused Raf of trying to fix the past. He couldn't. No more than she could change hers. She needed to forgive it, though. Forgive it and move on. But she didn't know how. And until she did, she would always try to turn her father into someone he could never be. Her dad would never accept Raf or his family.

But she wanted him to.

She went back into the kitchen and grabbed her phone. In seconds, her father's cell was ringing.

"Ember Rose, I'm at work. Is this about your mother?" No soft greetings of hello or excited words because it was her. He would do the same to her sisters, except he might show a little more warmth to Petra. He'd show even less to Nyx. Nyx was his last chance at a boy. Not only had she turned out to be a girl, but she was a sassy girl who loved all things that drove Huck mad. She made herself a country singer, changed her last name, and got a hold of a little fame just to piss their father off more. She envied Nyx her ability to tell Huck to shove it.

"Hello, Dad. No, I'm not calling about Mom. I was

wondering if I could talk to you for a few minutes about something else."

"Sure. Sure. But not now. I'll call you back when I get a break. Okay?"

"Yeah, okay. Thanks, Dad." At least he hadn't said no.

"Don't thank me yet. I haven't heard what you have to say." He ended the call.

He wouldn't like it when he did. Maybe she should have had this conversation before she and Raf had another fight. She could be putting herself in the line of fire for nothing.

Or for everything.

CHAPTER TWENTY-SEVEN

Raf pulled over and banged the steering wheel. His jaw hurt from clenching it. If Ember didn't understand how important it was to him to keep Tino from ruining his life, then how could they be together? She would have to accept that Tino would always be an important part of his life. In some ways, more important —well, maybe just important in a different way—than Matt or Ax.

He had raised Tino. He was more Tino's father than Johnny was. Tino was the five-year-old who climbed into his lap and gave him books and said, "Read, Raffy. Read."

Tino was also the middle schooler who played pranks on his teachers and got in trouble. Or the high schooler who flipped desks, cut class, smoked on school grounds, stole from his classmates' lockers, and crashed cars that didn't belong to him.

He hadn't been enough for Tino. He had tried, but becoming a dad at eighteen did not qualify him for the role. He was a kid himself, trying to raise a child and guide Matt and Ax through the end of their teen years.

Tino had not found a good outlet for his anger. Not like Ax, who had spray-painted everything with a flat surface. All that angry painting had turned him into an amazing artist who paved the way for others like him.

He picked up the phone and dialed Tino's number.

"Hey, big brother. How's it going?" Tino's voice was light and welcoming, as if none of their problems had transpired between them recently.

"Where were you last night?"

"I crashed at a friend's. I told Johnny to tell you."

"Don't lie to me, Santino. You walked out while we were unloading boxes from the spare bedroom. Whose couch did you land on?"

"Man, what difference does it make? I'm back now. I just didn't want to do any more work, so I took off. No big deal."

"You can't disappear and not tell anyone."

"I'm sick of you sounding like my father. Johnny's back. I don't need you anymore."

The words were a punch to the face. He took a deep breath to recover. "Good. Because I'm tired of taking care of your useless ass. Let Johnny clean up your messes. You should be making one anytime now."

"Are you done yelling at me? Because if all you want is to remind me what a piece of shit I am, I have to go."

"There's one more thing."

"Yeah? What's that?"

"Stay away from Ember." He ended the call before Tino could say another word. His phone lit back up instantly with Tino's name on the screen.

He declined the call and pulled back into traffic. If Tino wanted Johnny so badly and could disregard all that Raf had done for him, then Tino could have him.

Ember was right, but he didn't like it. He had to wipe his hands of Tino once and for all. And still he wanted to turn his truck around, go back to the house, and shake some sense into his brother.

If he thought it would work, he would beg; he would tear off a limb to make Tino act like a man. To be responsible. To hang up his anger and let the past go. They may not have had Johnny. But the four Alvarez brothers had each other. Why wasn't that enough for Tino?

Ember piled all her things by the front door. She would write Raf a goodbye note and leave it where he couldn't miss it. She had considered staying until the cookies were baked, but it might be better if she left and baked somewhere else. The question was, where?

She could drive the hour to Petra's house and crash there for a few days, but Petra's life didn't work when something threw off her schedule. Petra would run around the house clucking and she would feel guilty for getting in the way. She also didn't want to drive the hour back to the alpaca farm from Petra's once the cookies were done to deliver them. Clearly, Petra's house was out.

Baking at her parents' house was an option. She could call her father and tell him she was coming. She could swear not to talk to her mom about anything other than cookies. He might say no. He would have no problem denying her access to his stoves for her little business venture. He would probably want to know how she was paying for all her supplies and her living expenses without a real job.

He would have a point. She could live off her savings which she hadn't planned, but now saw as her best option. Then she would have to find a place to live with a good kitchen. A kitchen like Raf's.

Her phone buzzed in her pocket. She dug it out to find a text from Raf.

Will you be at my house when I get back?

She noted the absence of the word *home*. Something he had said just the day before. She stared at the screen, unsure of how to respond. He wasn't throwing her out. She had been the one to pack her belongings and head for the hills. Running—just as he had accused her. She had nowhere to go. Still, her fingers refused to type back.

The bubble of dots appeared on the screen.

I just want to talk. Will you be there?

She held her breath. *Okay.* She shoved her phone back in her pocket, grabbed her box of baking supplies, and went into the kitchen to get to work.

The afternoon ticked by while she became lost in the smell of sweet ingredients and the results of her hard work. With the last of the cookies in the oven, Ember wiped the counter down. Her low back ached from all the standing, but it was a good ache. She had accomplished something important today. Her first batch of cookies for a customer was almost boxed and ready to go. She had even decided on the three cookies she would specialize in first. That tingle of excitement tickled her belly like seltzer. She had never felt this way about work before.

She stole a glance at the clock above the sink. Raf would be back in an hour, and then they would have their talk. She expected the *it's not you, it's me* speech. He would take the burden of the breakup because that was the kind of man he was. But she knew in her heart that unless she gave her blessings for him to coddle Tino, they could not be together. He wasn't ready to make space in his life for a serious commitment while he still carried the guilt of Tino's choices.

Her phone rang from the other side of the kitchen where she had left it earlier. She dropped the sponge and reached for the phone. Her mother's name popped up on the screen.

"Hi, Mom."

"Ember. Ember. Ember." Her mother's voice screeched and shattered like a million pieces of crystal hitting the floor.

Her heart stuck in her throat. "What's the matter?"

"Come quick. Your father shot a man."

CHAPTER TWENTY-EIGHT

Ember raced through the front door of her parents' house. Her feet tangled on the wrinkled rug by the door and she tripped, righting herself before her chin clocked the table against the wall.

"Mom? Dad?" She slid to a stop in the kitchen. "Holy…"

The back door was open and the glass had been broken and scattered on the floor. The breeze pushed the door back and forth on its creaking hinges.

Her mother sat at the kitchen table with her bloodied hands in her lap. Her face was translucent. The veins in her cheeks were like blue road maps leading to her mouth hanging open. Her eyes were vacant.

Her father stood in the corner with a pistol in his hand. Her stomach heaved and she clamped her lips down to keep from vomiting.

Tino Alvarez sat on the floor, legs spread out in front of him, bleeding through a dish towel wrapped around his thigh and gritting his teeth. The color had drained from his face too. His eyes were watery and sweat poured down from his scalp. He shook as he held the towel to his leg. The smell of iron permeated the air.

"You shot him?" Even with the scene in front of her, she couldn't believe her eyes. She gripped the wall for balance.

"He broke into my house and tried to steal from us. He's lucky I didn't shoot him in the heart." Her father's face was red and the vein on the side of his neck pulsed like an angry serpent.

"I'm lucky you're a bad shot," Tino said through that clenched jaw.

"Shut up." Huck pointed the gun at Tino.

"Dad, put the gun down." Her breathing came in short, quick bursts. Her heart beat as if it were ice in a drink shaker.

"I don't feel so well," Mom said.

"Ruby, put your head between your legs. The sheriff will be here in a minute. And this scum will finally go to jail." Dad pointed the gun at the floor, but his burning gaze never wavered.

"You're going to prison for shooting me. I didn't do anything wrong." Tino's chest heaved and sweat ran down his face.

Her father let loose a menacing laugh that sent shivers down her spine. Her father wouldn't spend a second in jail. But Tino could no matter what he did or didn't do. She didn't know what to do. She should call Raf and have him come. Maybe she should call her uncle Silas to help.

Instead, she knelt down in front of Tino, needing to know the truth. "Did you steal from us?"

He met her gaze. "And what if I did? So what?"

Chaos burst into the house and she jumped away from Tino as the police and paramedics stormed the kitchen. The paramedics helped Tino. The sheriff took the gun from her father and escorted him out of the house like two friends on a stroll. A female paramedic spoke softly to her mother.

"I'd like to take her in for observation," the paramedic said to Ember.

"No." Mom pushed out of the chair hard enough to knock it back and held up her hands. "I want to stay in my home with my daughter. I can't go to the hospital." Her gaze darted around the room as if searching for more danger that could be anywhere. And it was, wasn't it?

"It's okay," she said. "I'll take care of her."

Raf jumped out of the elevator and tore down the hospital hallway. Someone had called the main line at the orchard, looking for him. It had been Brad that found him in the fields and delivered the news that Huck had shot Tino because Tino tried to take money and valuables out of Huck's home.

"I'll wait here," Brad said from the end of the hall.

"Thanks," he shouted over his shoulder. Brad had insisted he drive to keep Raf from maybe killing himself on the ride over. That was what family did. Family didn't hurt the people they cared about.

A police officer stood outside one of the rooms. That had to be Tino's. "My brother is in there."

The officer only nodded.

He flew through the door. Johnny sat in a chair in the corner with his lips pressed into a thin line. Fatigue masked his face. He shook his head as Raf stood before him. Neither one of them spoke.

Tino was handcuffed to the bed. His leg was in a cast and elevated. Tino had aged ten years since he saw him last. Served him right. Maybe he'd grow up.

"How could you?" His voice shook with fury and hurt and fear. The pain was soul crushing. Tino could have died or he could have hurt Ruby if Huck hadn't left work early and been there when his stupid brother tried to steal again.

Tino turned his face away.

"Look at me. Why would you steal from Ruby and Huck? I don't understand you." Unexpected tears burned behind his eyes. He had devoted his adult life to taking care of his brother. The hours spent worrying about each and every decision he made had left scars on his heart. And yet, no matter what he had done, Tino was determined to destroy himself.

Tino turned back. The light went out of his eyes as if a switch had been thrown, and he stared with a cold, empty hardness. "Don't you want to ask how I'm feeling?"

"No. I don't care. I need to know why you continue to try and ruin the things that are important to me. Stealing from the orchard was bad enough. But to break into the home of the parents of the woman I care for… Please make me understand."

"Rafael, maybe now isn't the time." Johnny stood and reached a hand out.

He brushed his father away. "Oh no. He's not getting off that easily. Not this time. I want to know why you do what you do. Tell me, damn it." He couldn't control the rise of his voice or the pain snaking up through his throat.

"I don't know."

"That's it? That's all you've got? I need more than *I don't know*, Santino."

"I don't know why I do it. I'm broken, I guess. I'm not like you and the others." Tino clenched his jaw. The trademark move Raf had witnessed Tino's entire life. Most often when Tino didn't want Raf to see him upset.

"That's bullshit and you know it." He leaned in and yelled in Tino's face.

"Okay. I'll tell you." Tino lunged from the bed, but the handcuffs pulled him back. "I hate that the orchard means so much to you. It's just a bunch of stupid trees. And I hate that you picked Ember over me. You moved her into your house when you wanted to throw me out."

"Because you stole from the orchard." He threw his hands in the air, wanting to make this merry-go-round of a conversation stop. It wasn't the job that Tino was so angry about. It was more. Much more, but until Tino realized that, there was nothing left for him to do.

"I'm out of here." He turned to go.

"Raf, wait." Tino's voice pleaded.

"What?" He hesitated as old habits died hard.

"You can't let me go to prison." Tino shook his hand shackled to the side of the bed. "Please do something. Talk to Huck. I didn't actually take anything. I mean, okay, I did break the glass on the door and let myself in the house, but he shot me before I could take anything."

"Dios mio," Johnny said.

"I can't help you this time." He should have let Tino go to jail a long time ago. Maybe a night or two in juvie would have straightened him out and he never would have come this far.

"Raf, please. I won't last in prison. I'll go away longer this time."

"Not my problem anymore." He turned for the door again. Tino yelled something after him, but he blocked it out. Tino's screams followed him down the hall. He faltered once, desperately wanting to turn around and drag his brother into his arms, but he pushed forward on shaking legs.

Brad waited for him by the elevator just like he said he would. "How'd it go?"

"Pretty bad." He called for the elevator.

Brad patted him on the shoulder. "I'm sorry."

"You can say I told you so." The doors opened, and they stepped inside.

"Why would I do that?" Brad shoved his hands into his pockets.

"Because you were right about Tino. I should have sent him to jail when you caught him keeping money from the applesauce orders."

"I've got nothing to say. Don't even know what you're talking about." Brad rocked on his heels.

"Thanks. I appreciate it." He couldn't meet Brad's gaze. The shame still burned fierce through his veins. "I wish I had a family like yours."

"Nah. We're nothing special. Besides, we have Huck." Brad choked out a laugh. The elevator doors opened. "Where to next?" Brad said.

"Drop me home. I'll get my truck later." He wanted a cold beer and for this day to be over.

"Will Ember be there?" They pushed through the glass doors and into the evening air.

"Would you be if you were her?"

"I see your point."

CHAPTER TWENTY-NINE

R af hopped out of Brad's truck and tapped the roof as Brad drove away, leaving him alone. Only he wasn't completely alone.

Ember carried a shipping box with the flaps bobbing up and down to her car. He hadn't expected her to be here at all. At least he could say goodbye.

"Hey," was all he could manage.

"I didn't think you'd be back so soon. I'll be gone in a few minutes if you could just give me that and wait out back so I don't have to see you." Each word seemed to get caught on the hiccup of her emotions.

"I'm sorry." He wanted to reach for her and make her feel better. He wanted to erase the pain etched on her face and wipe away the dark circles under her beautiful blue eyes. But he stayed put, keeping himself a safe distance from her. She must be disgusted by him and his brother. And she would have every right to be.

"Yeah, me too." She dropped her gaze to the box.

"Ember, I told Tino I wouldn't help him this time. He

has to pay for his mistakes on his own. He's going to jail for this." It would have been so easy to ask Brad to get involved on his behalf. Together they could have convinced Huck to let Tino go. But he had made that mistake before, and he would never do it again. Because next time someone would end up dead.

"I guess better late than never. Would you excuse me?" She brushed past him.

Headlights turned into the driveway, blinding him for a second. The lights extinguished and he could make out Johnny's car. Johnny pulled around Ember, not blocking her in, and got out. He nodded and went inside.

"Do you want help with your boxes?" he said.

"No, thank you. I'm almost done."

"Okay, then. I'll wait out back for you to finish. Take your time." He wanted to kiss her or wrap her in his arms once more. Instead, he fisted his hands at his sides and walked away.

He dropped down on the back step because he hadn't brought out any of the patio furniture yet. He stared at the shed. He might have to burn that thing to the ground because now every time he went in there he'd picture making love to Ember on his sleeping bag. He may never carve another piece of wood as long as he lived.

The back door to Johnny's side of the house slid open. He came out and sat on the steps by his door. His legs, long like Raf's, bent at the knees and came close to his shoulders. Just like Raf's. He and his dad were cut from the same mold physically, but Johnny and Tino shared the same mold when it came to letting people down.

"Clear night," Johnny said, looking up at the sky. He

pulled a pack of cigarettes out of his shirt pocket and lit up.

"I guess."

"Are you okay?" Johnny took a drag on the cigarette.

"I'd rather not talk." There were no more words. What was done was done. He'd have to find a way to move forward and let all of this go somehow. He might actually have to quit the orchard too. He blamed Tino for robbing Huck and Ruby, but what if Huck had killed his brother? Too much water and all that.

"I think you should talk," Johnny said. "It helps."

"I don't care what you think. It's your fault all this happened." The anger reared its ugly head. He wanted to blame Johnny for all their problems. He wanted to blame himself too.

"You're right."

"Excuse me?"

"You're right. I set this ball in motion. I set it in motion the minute I made your mother pregnant with you. I can't unring that bell. I don't even want to. I made four wonderful boys. They deserved better than me, but the pride I feel when I see you four. A father couldn't ask for more."

"You're proud of Tino?"

"I'm not proud of what he's done. But his actions aren't him. He's still that sweet boy who liked to dance in the kitchen when we played the radio. Do you remember that?" A thin smile pulled on Johnny's lips.

A warmth in his heart betrayed him. "Yeah. He was so goofy in that saggy diaper, jumping in circles. But that's not him anymore."

"You're wrong."

He jumped up. "No, you're wrong. Tino tried to hurt the family of the woman I love. That little boy went away the same day you did. You stole him. And I had tried to bring him back. I tried to protect him and make him whole. I tried to be enough of a parent for him, but I wasn't. I failed my little brother. I failed him over and over by trying to protect him from his feelings. From all the feelings of anger he carries around because his father didn't love him enough to stay."

The words stuck in his throat. The tears returned. He would not cry in front of this man. He would have been glad to let loose the river of emotions with Silas standing before him, but not Johnny Alvarez. Never Johnny Alvarez.

Johnny approached him with slow, steady steps. "I do love him. I love you all. And I did a very bad job of showing it. But I'm better now. That's why I'm here. I want to make up for what I did. I want to set things right as best I can. But you have to forgive the past and your-self, or you will never be happy."

He held his breath and stared Johnny straight in the eye. "I can't. I've lost Ember for good because of Tino. Huck hated us before. Now he has a reason to hate us. She'll never be able to stand up to her father and tell him that she cares for me. She cared for me, anyway. That's over now."

"Her feelings for you haven't changed."

"How do you know that?"

"Because you are a good man with a tender soul. Because you care so deeply it hurts you. You are honest and true and a healer. A woman would be a fool not to love you."

His father had never said such kind words to him. He had said the opposite many times when he was growing up. It seemed as if now Johnny was finally able to reach down and open his heart.

"I appreciate the pep talk, but she and I are through."

"Give her time."

He sat back down on the step and this time Johnny sat beside him. "None of this is your fault, Rafael."

"Then how come it feels like it is?"

"Give yourself time too." Johnny patted him on the knee. "How about some dinner, you and me? I'll cook. You bring the beer. What do you say?"

He met Johnny's gaze. This was not the man who had walked out on them. That man was glassy-eyed and angry. He was sad and desperate. This man with him tonight had clear eyes and radiated strength. This was the man he needed growing up. He couldn't go back in time and find that man for that boy.

But he could let the past go and rebuild the future with a bridge built on forgiveness.

"I'd love to have dinner with you. I'll get the drinks."

Johnny put his arm around his shoulders and pulled him to his side. "Excellent."

It kind of was.

CHAPTER THIRTY

The knocking shook Ember from her sleep. It took a second to remember she was on the couch at her parents' house and not in bed beside Raf. After she had left his place, she had driven here without thinking. Her father had pulled the door open and let her in without a word. What was there to say anyway? At least her mother was not hurt and nothing had been taken because her father had returned home early from work.

Last night, she had fallen asleep on the couch. Her old room was now empty. No remnant of her remained. Her father had packed up her things and put them in the attic twenty years ago, and there they still sat.

Her father had been right about Tino, and Raf had been right about Tino too. She had been the one who thought he deserved to be treated like an adult, and she had been wrong. She had been so wrong that she lost Raf over it because she had told him to stop trying to take care of his brother. But Raf understood Tino way better.

The knocking continued with some urgency. She glanced at her phone. It was just past seven in the morning. Who could be banging on the door, and where was her father? Wasn't he going to work today? He should be the one answering the door.

She threw back the blanket and steadied herself on sleep-deprived legs. Maybe it was Raf. If by some miracle it was, she would tell him how sorry she was for judging his choices concerning his family. She should have listened to him and never taken a ride from Tino. Tino had used her. All those questions had been to gather information, not out of kindness the way Raf would have asked.

The doorbell rang its shrill tune. She flung the door open, hoping to stop the noise. Her stomach dropped. It wasn't Raf.

"Johnny, what are you doing here?"

"I'm sorry it's so early, but I was hoping to speak with you and your father for a brief moment." Johnny's eyes were puffy and the hair on his jawline was thicker than he normally wore it. But a sadness had fallen over him, hunching his shoulders and making him look older than he really was.

"Take a hike, Alvarez. I don't want the likes of you on my property." Her father came up behind her and stood by her shoulder. He smelled of minty aftershave. The same aftershave he had worn her whole life.

"I understand. This will only take a second."

"Get off my porch before I call the cops."

"Dad, please. Let him speak." She wanted to hear what he had to say. If for no other reason than she could see Raf in the shape of his face and the curl to his lip when he smiled. Her heart ached for the man she lost.

"I came to apologize for my son. He needs to apologize too, but I want you to know that I also take blame for him. It is because I left him when he was a little boy and he had to be raised by his older brother. Santino is angry at me, and he takes it out on the world. It's no excuse. He must be responsible for his actions. I hope you will understand that my son has problems. Someday, maybe, he will get well."

"You're all alike," her father said. "You and your sons. If having sons means having men who can't be trusted, I'll stick with my girls."

"Dad, enough. Johnny came here in good faith." Somewhere inside her father's complaints was a compliment to her and her sisters.

"Good faith, my ass. He doesn't want me to sue him." Huck marched away, swinging his arms in the air. And she had hoped he was softening. She was expecting too much.

"Please forgive my father. It's been a rough time for him."

"No forgiveness is necessary. May I speak to you outside for a moment?" Johnny hitched a thumb over his shoulder.

She was in her pajamas, and her mouth tasted like dirt. She must look a fright from attempting to sleep on the most uncomfortable couch ever. And with all that, she wasn't sure there was much else to say, but he gazed at her in earnest.

"Okay." She followed him out on the porch and down

the drive to lean on his car. "My son cares very much for you."

"Johnny, I don't think you and I should be discussing this. Raf and I... well, I guess we just have bad timing or something."

"Please don't hold Santino's actions against Rafael. He's a good man."

"Tino tried to rob us. How do we move on from that?"

"With love. Love for each other and understanding for Santino who hopefully will get help this time."

"And if he doesn't?"

"Talk to Rafael. I only came to pay respects to your family. And... to encourage you not to miss out on something that could be beautiful." He gave her a sideways smile. "Rafael will be home all day. He took the day off work. It might have even been the week." Johnny shrugged, got in his car, and drove away as if he'd never been there at all.

She headed back inside. Her father waited on the other side of the door with his arms over his chest. "What did he want to say to you?"

She met her father's gaze. She could lie or avoid the question. Or she could tell the truth. "He told me to give Raf another chance."

"How involved with him were you?"

"Very." Her belly warmed at just the thought of them together.

"You can't. That family is no good."

She didn't have to stay here and take this from him. No matter how much he budged, he would never change. He would always see the world from his small window.

"Here's the thing, Dad. You don't get a say. Just like I don't get a say as to whether or not I can be a part of Mom's care. She's made it clear she doesn't want me to see her decline. I have to live with that so I had better spend as much time with her as I can until she says no more." She pointed a finger at her father. "Just like you have to learn to live with the fact that I love Rafael Alvarez. He had a tough life, but he pulled through just fine. He's a wonderful man who works hard. And you know that, no matter how much you complain about him. So, get over it. I don't care what Tino did. I mean I do, but it doesn't define Raf."

She had said it all. Raf had been right about her running away from dealing with this. Her father would have to find a way to accept that she wanted Raf, more than anything.

"You and your sisters. Always doing what you want." He narrowed his eyes. "Only because my stubborn brother thinks the world of him, which I don't understand, mind you, but Silas is a pretty good judge of character. And Alvarez always gets to work on time, never complains, and the men in the field like him. My dimwitted nephew likes him too. So, I guess he's alright."

"Are you saying you like Raf?" She rubbed her ear to make sure she heard correctly.

"Let's not get crazy. But I won't say much if you two decide to date again."

"I don't know if that will happen. Maybe someday when all this calms down."

"But you just said you loved him."

"I do."

"Then what's the problem?"

What indeed?

~

Ember parked the car in the train station parking lot. The rental would have to be returned soon, and then she would need to buy a car of her own. Wherever she ended up living, if it was in New Jersey, she'd need a car to get around.

But today she was headed into the city. She had decided to take an accelerated baking course to help define her skills and add a little credibility to her business. Her father had offered to pay for it. How could she refuse?

She had attempted to call Raf several times, but she chickened out every time. She wanted to get her life in order first. And he hadn't called her either. It was probably for the better. They had been a flash in the pan kind of thing. Real love didn't burn that hot and fast. But she had sure hoped it did.

She slid out of the car with ten minutes before the train arrived. The weather was warm today. Summer teased the afternoon with balmy temperatures and bright sun.

"Excuse me, do you need a ride?" The familiar deep timbre of a male voice shook her to her core.

She soaked in Raf's presence from his black hair to his work boots and everything in between, landing squarely on that crooked smile. Her voice refused to work at first, but she swallowed and resurrected it. "No, thank you. I'm waiting for the train."

"Going away?" He kept his hands behind his back.

"Something like that. How did you find me here?" Her feet shifted, wanting to run to him, but she stayed in place.

"I stopped by your house. Your father said if I hurried I might catch you in time."

"My father gave my location away?"

"Miracles never cease. He also said that if I hurt you, he'd do a better job of shooting me." His top lip curled up further.

She couldn't help it, she laughed. "Oh, that's not funny."

"It kind of is." He smirked.

"How is Tino?" She was trying to forgive the past and build a new future. If she was really going to move in that direction, asking after his brother was the right thing to do.

"He'll be fine. He's going to spend some time in prison for breaking and entering and attempted robbery. I didn't come here to talk about Tino."

"What then?" The train would be there soon. She wished there was more time.

"I'm sorry, Ember. I'm sorry for everything. For the fight, for Tino hurting your mom. For not listening to you. I should have let Tino be a man. Instead, I made him into a thief."

She couldn't stay away and moved closer to him. "No, you didn't. He did that. You showed him how to be a man. You're the best man I know."

"I don't know about that."

"Stop it. Just stop it. You have the biggest heart. You take care of everyone, including me. And I didn't deserve it. I should have been firmer with my father about us.

And I shouldn't have allowed Tino to drive me home when you told me not to."

The train whistled in the distance. Their time was running out. "I need to say something," she said.

"So do I."

"Please let me go first."

"Okay."

"I'm sorry too. I threw myself into your life without thinking and messed everything up. At least, I finally told my father how I felt about you even though it was too late."

The ground rumbled as the train came closer.

"I figured you might have when he was actually pleasant to me." He inched closer to her. The train slowed as it approached the platform. The hissing brakes fought against the girth of the metal cars.

"I have to get on that train." But she didn't want to. She wanted more time to speak with him.

"I just wanted to say that if you would consider giving me another chance, I would make sure Tino stays out of our lives until I know he's changed. I won't ever let him hurt you again. I swear it. I'd die first."

His words were honest, because Raf did not lie. He would not hurt her on purpose, if ever. Together they could figure out what to do with their families. But the words in her mouth stayed quiet. She would think before she spoke this time.

The conductor announced that all passengers should board the train.

"I brought you something. I hope you'll keep it, even if you don't want to see me anymore." He pulled his hand out from behind his back and presented a bunny carved from wood. "You mentioned you like rabbits." He shrugged.

She hurled herself into his arms, practically knocking the bunny loose and him over. So much for thinking first.

He scooped her up and held her close. He smelled like wood and musk. She sank against him. He had said he would carve a bunny for her the night they made love in the shed. He was the most thoughtful person she knew.

"Ma'am, are you getting on this train?" The conductor said, interrupting them.

"She just needs a minute." Raf released her and steadied her on her feet.

The conductor tapped his watch with an impatient look on his face.

"When's the next one?" She could be a little late. Or she could start tomorrow. She took the rabbit and turned it around in her hands. It was perfect.

"In an hour," the conductor said.

"Leave without me." She turned to Raf. "Thank you for this."

"I didn't think it would turn out so well. It's not even my best."

"You can make me more."

"Then I guess that's a yes."

"A yes?" What was he saying? She might be the one who leaped first and thought second, but not him. He wouldn't rush into a proposal, still her breath hitched at the idea.

"A yes to us. To you moving back into my house. To a future together."

"Absolutely a yes." She took his hand, and they

walked toward his truck. Amazing how life could change with one impulsive decision. If she had thought at all about what she was doing the day she bolted out of her apartment, she would not have bumped into Raf.

"You should catch the next train," he said.

"You don't even know where I was going."

"Oh, your dad told me that too." He laughed and squeezed her hand. "I won't let you miss your first day of baking school. But I'd like to make the most of the hour we have." He arched a brow.

"So, you weren't worried I was meeting someone?" She relished the idea of a little time together in the back of his truck. That wasn't too impulsive—was it?

"I thought maybe you were going back to the city for good. That maybe that ex of yours was waiting. But not after I handed you that carving. Then I knew I still had a chance."

"I love you, Rafael. I loved you from the first minute I laid eyes on you. I didn't know it that day. But I do now. You restored my soul." She placed a kiss on his lips.

"And I love you, Ember. I love the way you run full force at life. I want you to know that no matter what happens with your mom, or anything in your life, I will stand by your side every step of the way." He cupped her face.

"And I will do the same for you. I'm done running away, Raf. I've found my home with my sweet, sexy, benevolent man."

Then he kissed her.

ALSO BY STACEY WILK

Serenity Series

Sea Glass Made with Second Chances

Sea Glass Hidden in Plain Sight

Sea Glass Out of Balance

Sea Glass Wrapped in Red

<u>Heritage River Series</u>

The Risk for House and Home

The Bridge Between Love and Lies

The Essence of Whiskey and Tea

<u>Hometown Series</u>

Taking Root

Raising Winter

Defining Chances

Beginning Over

Steeling Hearts

Whispering Christmas

Winter at the Shore Series

No More Darkness

Through the Darkness

Light Upon the Darkness

The Brotherhood Protectors World

Winter's Last Chance

The Last Betrayal

Her Last Word

The Last Days of Christmas

Seduced by Denial

Chill in the Air

Fighting for Tessa

Nash's Promise

Cruz's Watch

Harlan Unleashed

<u>Big Sky Country Series</u>

Time Won't Erase

Stay Awhile

Love Never Ends

Dare to Tell (coming soon)

READY FOR ANOTHER TRIP TO CANDLEWOOD FALLS?

Enjoy these exciting Spring 2022 Releases!

Can a bad boy help a good girl overcome her fears to find true love? Wilde in Love by KM Fawcett

Where broken dreams collide, two hearts will come together and find the love they thought they lost. It's in His Kiss by USA Today best selling author Jen Talty

ACKNOWLEDGMENTS

I would like to thank the people who helped me make this book better. First to Lori Matthews and Kimberley Ash for the invaluable feedback during the developmental stage of this story.

As always, a huge thanks to Robin Rottner for her input and suggestions. Robin, I don't know what I would do without you on this long journey.

A special thanks to the reader who helped me figure out how Tino stole from the orchard. She would like to remain anonymous for obvious reasons.

A wave of gratitude to my partners Jen and Kathy. I spend more hours with you two than I do the Coffee King some weeks!

Most importantly, I have to thank you, my readers. I am humbled each and every time you choose my books. Thank you for sharing your free time with me. I hope I have given you a chance to escape real life and find a little romance along the way.

~

ABOUT THE AUTHOR

From an early age, best selling author Stacey Wilk told tales as a way to escape. At six she wrote short stories in composition notebooks, at twelve she wrote a novel on a typewriter, in high school biology she wrote rock star romances in her binder instead of paying attention.

But it wasn't until many years later, inspired by her children and a looming birthday, that she finally took her story-telling seriously. And published her first novel in 2013. Since then, she's gone on to publish thirty-one more so women everywhere could fall in love and find an escape of their own.

She isn't done telling stories. Not by a long shot. If you want to read her best selling, emotional, and honest books about family, romance, and second chances, visit her at www.staceywilk.com

~